UNDYING CAVES

MERROW RUINS

THE FORBIDDEN CITY

OBSIDIAN WELL

CAVERNS OF MADNESS

RIMOROSA'S LAIR

SONG of the DEEP

BRIAN HASTINGS

STERLING CHILDREN'S BOOKS
New York

STERLING CHILDREN'S BOOKS
New York

An Imprint of Sterling Publishing Co., Inc.
1166 Avenue of the Americas
New York, NY 10036

ISBN 978-1-4549-2096-0

Distributed in Canada by Sterling Publishing Co., Inc.
c/o Canadian Manda Group, 664 Annette Street
Toronto, Ontario, Canada M6S 2C8
Distributed in the United Kingdom by GMC Distribution Services
Castle Place, 166 High Street, Lewes, East Sussex, England BN7 1XU
Distributed in Australia by Capricorn Link (Australia) Pty. Ltd.
P.O. Box 704, Windsor, NSW 2756, Australia

For information about custom editions, special sales, and premium and corporate purchases, please contact Sterling Special Sales at 800-805-5489 or specialsales@sterlingpublishing.com.

Manufactured in the United States of America
Lot #:
2 4 6 8 10 9 7 5 3 1
05/16

www.sterlingpublishing.com

Text by Brian Hastings

Illustrations by Alexis Seabrook

Images on title page, dedication page, pages 13, 34–35, 41, 42–43, 92–93, and 168 provided by Insomniac Games, Inc.

Interior design by Lorie Pagnozzi

FOR FIONA THE ARTIST AND
PATRICK THE ARCHITECT

LETTER FROM THE AUTHOR

When I first started thinking about the story for *Song of the Deep*, I wanted to create a hero for my daughter to look up to. I had noticed that when she told me about the female characters she liked in movies, she would almost always start by saying how pretty they were. Being pretty had even become a big part of her own identity. She tended to receive more compliments on her appearance than for being artistic, kind, funny, smart, or hardworking. I wanted to make a story for her where the main character was heroic and memorable only because of her inner qualities. And that's how Merryn first came to be.

For me, writing this book was a journey in itself. As a child I had always wanted to be an author. After college I got a job programming video games, and for twenty-one years I've been lucky enough to help create worlds and characters that are loved by millions of people. Over time I had forgotten my dreams of being an author. So when the opportunity came to write a book in conjunction with our latest game, it was both exciting and terrifying. I had written game stories before, but the idea of writing an actual novel now seemed impossibly daunting.

In the end, it was an incredible experience. It forced me to think about the things I value most and the kind of person I want to be. I even got a little emotional as I wrote the final chapters. Merryn is a character I didn't want to say goodbye to. I hope her journey is one that you will enjoy and remember as well.

—BRIAN HASTINGS

SONGS AND SECRETS

The first light of morning is seeping through my seashell curtains. I look down at the waves below my window. Today will be the day.

I hurry out of bed and throw on an old striped shirt and shorts. Pulling on my orange felt boots, I see my toes peeking through the ends. I'll have to remember to sew them up tonight. It's windy out there, so I put on my big blue jacket with the shiny gold buttons. One last thing: my sailor's hat. Etched on the front is an upside-down anchor that looks like the letter *M*.

There's no way he can say *no* today.

I hurry into the kitchen. My father gives me a smile as he hands me a slice of bread with honey. He knows the game we're about to play.

"Good morning, Dandelion."

"Morning, Daddy!" The bread tastes delicious. I can see he's eating his own slice plain, so I offer a bite of mine. He takes a step back, pretending to be afraid of it.

"We sailors can't touch sweets. It attracts the sea monsters, you know."

I keep eating. "Did you notice the holes in your nets are all fixed?"

"I saw that. Must have been sea pixies. I think I heard them rustling about last night."

"And remember how the rudder kept sticking to the left?"

"I do."

"Not anymore."

"Really?"

I smile. He has to say *yes* today.

"How are you learning all this?" he asks.

"Library books," I answer. He raises an eyebrow at me. "And the sea pixies help sometimes . . . mostly they're pretty lazy, though."

"Well, it *is* summer. Maybe they need to take a break and enjoy themselves," he replies. But I'm not going to give up that easily.

"Please, can I come out with you today?"

"Merryn, the sea is dangerous enough for someone as big as me. It's cold and it's windy and there are waves taller than our house. It's not safe for you to be out there."

"Maybe I'll bring you luck. You might catch twice as many fish with me there."

He looks down for a moment, and suddenly I feel bad. I know it's been a slow month, and there seem to be fewer and fewer fish each day. I change the subject.

"Have you seen the garden?"

"Yes, it's beautiful. I've never seen tomatoes so big."

"Be careful out there today," I say. I give him a hug and then wave good-bye as he heads out the door and down the steps toward the shore.

Our house sits at the edge of a cliff, one hundred feet above the sea. Winding rocky steps lead down to a patch of sand where my father docks his small wooden fishing boat. We have a beautiful view of the sea to the west; on a clear day I can see tiny islands in the far distance. Behind our house are two acres of green garden where I can plant anything I want. Beyond the garden is an old dirt road that leads out toward town, but there's never anyone on it. The nearest house is more than a mile away, and no people come out to our road unless they're lost.

I walk outside toward the cliff edge. Down below I see my father's boat heading out into the sea. I pick up a rock and toss it gently down toward the waves below. My friend Bree and I used to sit and talk for hours at the edge of this cliff. We'd both throw rocks and watch which one made the farthest splash. We'd tell each other stories about pirates and hidden treasure. We'd hunt for frogs in the tall grass. Those summers seemed to go on for ages. I pick up another stone and roll it over in my hand. Bree has a lot of friends in town now, so she doesn't come out here as often.

I throw the stone as far as I can and watch it fall down, down, down until it disappears into the foam of a wave.

Turning around, I look out at the garden. It really does look beautiful. Row after row of leafy plants is decorated with big red and green tomatoes. The potatoes, turnips, and carrots all look healthy too. I start gathering up the soil around each potato plant to form tiny hills around the stems, so I'll have more potatoes by the end of the summer. When we get dry spells, I sometimes have to make the trip down the dirt road to the well twenty times per day just to keep the garden alive. But we've been getting rain the last two weeks, so today the soil is moist and everything is looking healthy. I gather up a handful of carrots and turnips and three of the biggest tomatoes to take back to the house.

I leave the vegetables on the table and walk back out to the cliffs to the north. The rocky steps are still slick from last night's rain. I'm extra careful today, because I scraped my knee on the steps yesterday, and my father doesn't want me using the steps at all. They're pretty steep and uneven, and there's no railing, so if you do lose your balance, you could fall all the way down to the rocks along the shore. I know all the broken steps and loose rocks by heart, so I'm not in any real danger. There's just one tricky part: I have to jump over a five-foot gap where the steps got washed out during a storm.

The gap proves to be a little trickier than usual today. The wind coming off the sea is blowing hard, and I need to jump straight into it to clear the gap. I take a tiny running start and push off from the very edge of the gap. My boots slide a little bit on the landing, but I clear the gap with room to spare. The rest of the way down is pretty easy. I lean close to the wall on the long straightaway where the stairs narrow down to a single boot's width. Rounding the last turn, I quicken my pace and hurry down over the jumble of boulders at the base of the stairs.

A huge white pelican sits on the edge of our dock. He looks over at me as I walk past, lifting up his wings as if he's going to fly away.

"It's just me, Fergus. You see me every single day."

He settles his wings back down and looks back out at the sea. My father always throws him a fish when he gets home—when he's caught one, that is.

The tide is in now, so there's only a narrow path of sand between the rocks and the water as I walk over to the work shed. It's not really a shed so much as a little wooden roof that covers the tools and the supplies we use for repairing the boat. It's also where

I keep all the treasures that my father brings home from the sea.

His nets catch all sorts of metal scraps and driftwood. Sometimes he brings home truly bizarre objects I've never seen before. He makes up stories about them, telling me how they were part of a forgotten world deep beneath the waves. Once he brought back a golden claw arm connected to a tangled mess of gears. It looked like somebody's weird failed invention. My father said it was part of a gem harvester that collected the precious jewels from the darkest sea caves and brought them to a hidden city of gold under the sea.

I've kept every treasure he has ever brought back. There are piles of metal and wood scraps and the remains of mysterious machines lined along the rock wall behind the shed. Sometimes I try to fix the old machines and figure out what they were used for. Today I don't need anything fancy. I'm working on a present as a surprise for my father.

It's a clam shovel, and it's almost done. It took a while to find a sturdy piece of wood that was just the right size. Now I just need to finish shaping the metal blade. If I had a way to heat the metal up, my work would be a lot easier, but I'm still making steady progress. I hammer the metal blade into a nice long groove. It's a little longer than my forearm, so it should be deep enough to reach the razor clams. I wedge the shovel blade into the wood and bolt it into place. I'll give it to him tomorrow morning.

It's starting to rain a little bit. I look back over at Fergus.

"See you tomorrow, lazy bird." He just turns away and looks back toward the sea, waiting for my father. It's starting to get dark as I make my way back up the cliff steps. I have the wind at my back as I jump the gap. Two feet to spare, easily.

Only the top of the sun is visible above the horizon. I get the candle from my room and light it. When my father is out past dark, I like to hold a candle up for him at the cliff edge to guide him home. I stand and watch for the lantern on his boat to come toward me, and he watches for the tiny light above the cliffs. I put the glass shield around the candle and walk out to the cliffs, watching the lights of the boats below.

My father's boat is one of the smallest ones out

there, with only a single lantern. I scan the sea for a single bobbing light and at last I see it. I wave my candle back and forth, and my father waves the lantern in return. I follow the light as it gets closer and closer to the shore and finally disappears behind the cliff edge.

Back inside, I start chopping up vegetables for a fish stew. I hear the wind howling outside and listen for my father's heavy steps up the cliff stairs. When he comes in his head is low, and I see his bag is empty. Sometimes on the windy days the fish are hard to catch.

"I was thinking of seashell soup, tonight. What do you think?" My smile seems to make him feel a little better, but he knows that seashell soup is something I make when there's nothing else to cook.

"That does sound tasty. Here, let me help." He takes the knife and starts chopping up the turnips. He won't admit it, but I can tell he doesn't like me using the sharp knives. I've known how to clean a fish since I was eight years old, but he still insists on doing it himself. I take one of the duller knives and start chopping up the carrots.

When the vegetables are cut, I add in some rosemary and thyme from the garden and a few colorful seashells and stir it up. We sit down at the table, each with our own bowl of seashell soup.

"It's like my own secret tide pool," I say, stirring up my soup and watching the seashells swirl around.

"Tastiest tide pool I've ever had. Must be something magic in your seasonings." He picks up one of the orange seashells with a spoon and holds it up as if he's thinking about something. I notice there's sadness in his eyes, and then I remember that it's June. He always gets a little sad at the start of summer. June is the month that my mother died.

It was seven years ago. I was only five years old when it happened. When I try to remember that day I can only see tiny fragments of it. I remember rowing out into the waves with her. I remember the sun shining in her dark hair. Everything else is just blank.

We finish our soup. I try to think of something to cheer up my father.

"Any sea monsters out there today?"

"Huge ones. Queen leviathans. Where do you think all those waves were coming from?"

"Good thing you didn't eat that honey."

"That's true. I saw three other boats get swallowed whole. Probably had marmalade aboard. Leviathans can't get enough marmalade."

"Speaking of leviathans, you haven't sung me a lullaby in a long time."

"Aren't you tired of hearing them?"

"Never."

He used to sing me lullabies every night. They were originally my mother's songs that she sang to me when I was a baby. I think she learned them from her own parents. The songs sound very old somehow, like they're from a different time. I don't remember the sound of my mother's voice, but my father's voice is deep and gravelly. Even so, there's a strange kind of beauty about the way he sings. When his voice catches on some of the notes, I know he's thinking about my mother.

As I'm getting ready for bed I start thinking about how each of the songs tells a story. When I was younger I actually believed they were all true.

The ancient explorers who conquered the sea and created underwater cities. The city of gold hidden at the bottom of the sea. The giant sea monsters that would snatch boats and leave their broken remains in a watery mountain of wreckage. Most of all I loved the stories of the brave merrow men and merrow maidens, half fish and half human, who defended the sea from those who stole its treasures.

I can't remember when I stopped believing in all of it. There was no single moment when I realized it was imaginary. Over time I just grew up, and I knew. But sometimes, like tonight, I wish I could still believe there was an undiscovered world of secrets out there. I wish I could listen to my father's songs and dream of exploring the unknown.

My father tucks me in and pulls up a chair by the side of my bed.

"Got to get an early start tomorrow, try to beat the winds."

"Just one song?"

"Hmmm . . . let's see. You might need to help me if I forget the words." He starts to hum a tune to himself to remember how it goes. Then he begins.

Beneath the wind and the
crashing waves

Lie merrow maidens and men so brave

Their tails are stronger than iron mail

They swim with the grace of
a billowing sail

Beyond the howl of the dragons deep

In the lightless caves where the
nightwyrm creep

They all will quake 'neath
the watching eye

The light will burn and the sea will dry

My father's voice is echoing and distant. For
a moment I feel that I am there, in that strange
undersea world . . . and then I am asleep.

2

THE CANDLE AT THE CLIFF

When I wake up, my father is already gone. I look out the window to see the sky is dark with rain clouds. It's going to be even worse weather than yesterday.

There's a slice of bread with honey waiting for me on the table. The honey is drizzled in the shape of a dandelion. As I eat, I remember the clam shovel. Even if there are no fish today, I can still surprise my father with a whole plate of clams.

I put on my coat, grab a bucket, and head down the cliff steps. The winds are stronger today. I have to wait for a pause in the gusts before I attempt to jump the gap. When I get to the bottom, I look out at the dock.

Even Fergus isn't out today. Maybe he was angry that there were no fish yesterday and went off to hunt for himself.

The storm clouds are looking darker already. I grab the clam shovel and set out along the shore. The tide is still out, so I've got a wide stretch of sand to search. I walk close to the waterline, looking for the tiny telltale holes. I find a pair of them right away. Putting all my weight on the shovel, I drive the blade into the sand. I lean on the handle to pull it up, and out pops my first razor clam. It's a big one, too, even longer than my hand. I put it in the bucket and keep going.

I've got five more clams in the bucket when I feel the first drops of rain in my hair. Seconds later, it's coming down in huge gusting sheets. I can't stop now. If I wait for the storm to end the tide will come in and I'll miss my chance. I run from hole to hole, scooping up clams. My hair is soaked all the way through by the time the bucket is half full, but it's more than enough for a good meal.

I dash back up the slippery cliff steps, leaning against the wind as I go. I hesitate as I get to the gap.

I'll have the wind with me, but now I'm carrying a bucket half full of razor clams. I won't be able to use my arms in the jump, and I can't get a solid running start because the path is slick with rain. Taking a few steps back, I wait for the wind to pick up. I clutch the bucket with both hands and run toward the gap, pushing off the edge as hard as I can. My foot slips on the edge, and I topple forward in mid-air.

I hit the ground hard on the other side, my legs sticking out over the gap and the clams spilling onto the rocky path. I scramble forward, away from the gap, and scoop up the clams. It looks like I lost a few over the edge, but I've still got plenty.

The rain pelts me as I climb the rest of the way up to the house. At the top of the stairs I look back out toward the sea. The waves are taller than I have ever seen before. I hope my father decides to come back early. I can't wait to see his face when he smells freshly steamed clams.

Back in my room, I watch the waves down below, looking for the bobbing lantern of my father's boat. I pick up my sketchbook and draw. I draw jagged towering cliffs that hang like an open jaw over the waves of the sea. I draw Fergus sitting on the dock, his mouth wide open like a trash can. My walls are covered in drawings. Looking from one side of the room to the other, you can see how my style evolved from happy yellow suns poking out of corners to brooding, charcoal-shaded portraiture. Lately I've been drawing seascapes. I try to make each one tell a story of the secrets that lie beneath the surface.

I keep restlessly looking back out the window. The wind is beating against the side of the house, making the door rattle in its frame. I look back down at my drawing and see that I've sketched a tiny boat, cradled by giant waves. I stop and stare up at the ceiling. There's a drawing there that I must have done when I was five years old. It shows my mother and father and me all playing and laughing in the waves as a smiling sea serpent swims in the background. That was the last picture I drew of my mother.

The rain is pouring harder than ever now. I'm starting to grow anxious. I light the candle and put on my jacket. Out at the cliff edge, I can barely see the white crests of the waves in the darkness. I cover the top of the glass shield with my hand to keep the rain off the candle. I watch the lights of the ships bobbing in the waves, knowing one of them must be my father.

One by one the lights turn to the left or to the right and then disappear. I hold the candle up high, hoping my father can see it through the rain. The sea is dark now. There are no more lantern lights on the waves. Maybe my father's light burnt out? Or maybe it was broken in the storm. I stare out at the blackness of the sea. And I wait.

The rain pours down, and I wait.

My legs shake from the cold and my soaking hair covers my eyes, but I keep the candle held up. I know he's out there somewhere, looking at my candle and trying to get home.

I wait.

I try to imagine his proud smile when he sees the clam shovel I made for him.

My arms ache from holding the candle up. I stare out into the darkness, listening to the distant crash of the waves. The candlelight is fainter now. The wax is almost gone.

The wind has died down. The rain is a constant, steady stream.

I wait.

The candle's tiny flame flickers and disappears. I'm in total darkness.

I kneel down at the cliff edge and stare out toward the sea, waiting for a light to appear.

I lie down for just a moment, resting my head on my arm.

I can hear my father's voice.

"Hold on to me, Merryn." I look around for him in the darkness. The ground is tipping under my feet. There are waves all around us. We're on the deck of his boat. My father pulls me toward the hatch, helping me get below deck. A huge wave crashes down over us. Water spills through the hatch, soaking my clothes.

I reach for my father's hand. Through the hatch I see something heavy and red crash onto the deck. My father is knocked backward and the hatch slams shut. I rush back up the ladder to reopen it. I can't believe what I'm seeing. There's a giant red tentacle arm wrapped around the hull of the boat.

The boat shakes violently back and forth. I lose my footing and fall down, banging my head on the floor. I hear my father's voice.

"Merryn! Merryn!" He's coming down the hatch. Suddenly we're pulled downward very fast. The sound of the wind is gone. Everything seems quiet. Water is rushing into the hatch, rising quickly inside the tiny cabin. My father picks me up and holds my head up as the water pours in. We're sinking. Not just sinking, but being violently pulled downward through the water.

My father's face disappears below the water in the boat. He's still holding my head above water. I reach for him. I grab his hands and try to pull him up with me.

And then I wake up.

I'm still lying on the ground at the edge of the cliff. The rain has stopped.

It wasn't just a dream. I can't explain how I know, but it was too real to be just a dream. I was there. My father was there. He's down below the waves right now and he needs my help.

I know what I have to do.

SCRAPS OF HOPE

I hurry down the cliff steps, leaping the gap without breaking my stride. In the shed I take inventory of everything I've got to work with. There are gleaming scraps of gold-colored metal, a few sturdy planks of wood, a half dome of glass, and piles of the strange mechanical contraptions that I can't even name. My father makes up some exotic explanation for each of the treasures he brings home. A half dome of glass was once a monocle for a giant cyclops octopus. A little propeller was a merry-go-round for playful hermit crabs.

I look back and forth at the jumble, trying to decide where to start. I grab the biggest pieces of metal and start hammering them into curves. Each one has to align perfectly, so I carefully measure them as I go. They're surprisingly malleable, as if they were made to be sculpted. When the biggest scraps are all laid out and curved into shape, I use a hammer and awl to poke careful rows of holes along the edges. I bolt each piece together, one by one, securing the bolts as tightly as I can.

I take a step back. Am I crazy to think this is going to work?

There isn't much metal left, so I start collecting the sturdiest pieces of wood I can find. I sketch out a design in the sand and make some quick calculations. I saw the wood into carefully measured lengths and nail them together. The wood fits snugly into the metal frame, forming a tight seal. The outer frame is starting to take shape.

As I check the seals on the bottom of the frame, I spot a tiny hole at the front of the hull. It's barely bigger than an inch in diameter, but I'm not sure I have enough metal left to patch it.

Sifting through the dwindling pile of treasures, I find a striped orange zephyr whelk. I hold the colorful seashell in my hand—it's about the size and shape of an ice cream cone. What was the song my father sang about this one? There was something special about zephyr whelks. I try to recall the melody, and then stop myself. What am I doing? My father needs me. Every second matters.

I wedge the zephyr whelk into the hole in the front of the hull as tightly as I can. It's not a perfect solution, but I'm in a hurry. Maybe the little seashell will bring me luck.

I glance back toward the sea. The sun is already high overhead, and I feel a wave of panic. How do I really know my father is down there? If he is, how long can he survive under the water? My whole plan suddenly feels foolish. I look out at the dock to see Fergus staring back at me.

"What should I do, Fergus?" The pelican turns away and looks toward the sea. He doesn't believe in me either. I feel a huge weight pressing down on me. What am I thinking? I'm twelve years old. I can't do this. I'm just going to get myself killed.

The wood-and-metal frame I've built looks like a big bathtub. How did I ever think I would be able to ride inside it, let alone use it to find my father? I suddenly feel more alone than I have ever felt. I wish my mother was here. I wish I had someone to tell me what I should do.

I close my eyes. A light wind blows gently through my hair. I listen to the soft sound of the surf reaching toward me up the shore. Then I feel a hand on my shoulder. My father! I want to whirl around and embrace him, but my body is frozen. I feel the hand gently stroke my hair. The smell of wild orchids surrounds me. I remember my mother used to make necklaces out of their purple petals, one for her and one for me. I feel long soft hair graze my back, and a gentle kiss in my hair. I turn around.

The beach is empty. The smell of wild orchids is gone. Even Fergus has disappeared.

But so have my doubts. I know what I need to do and I know I can do it.

Suddenly I'm working faster than I thought possible. My hands are moving in a blur, as if they already know what to do. I finish the roof, bolting everything tight and double-checking each seam. I pull a little propeller and an axle out of the scraps. The next step will require some parts I don't have, but I think I have a solution.

I race back up the cliff steps. My purple bicycle is leaning against the side of the house.

For just a moment I hesitate. I remember the pride on my father's face when he gave it to me on my seventh birthday. I think of how many months he must have saved to be able to afford it. It's a beautiful bike. Bree and I used to ride together, down the dirt road, past the rolling green hills to the ruins of the old stone church. This bicycle has seen its share of adventures. And now it's time for it to become something new.

I wheel it down the cliff steps. At the gap I have to lean down on my stomach, lowering the bike by the handlebars. I let go, wincing as it clatters on the rocks below.

It's okay. I just need its parts now.

Down at the shed I disassemble the bike piece by piece. I take the chain, pedals, and handlebars and start putting them together inside the frame. I find some old gears from the pile of treasures and bolt them in on little axles. The bicycle's seat goes in last. I adjust the height as best I can, but it's definitely a little cramped in there.

Next I take the curved half dome of glass and carefully maneuver it into the front of the frame. It shudders as it slides against the metal, but it locks solidly into place.

At last I bolt a hatch onto the roof. The hinges are old and rusty, but it'll do as a way to get in and out. A little voice in my head questions why I'd need to get out and how I'd do so, but I ignore it.

I step back and admire my work. It's tiny and it's rickety and some parts are a little rusty . . . but it's my very own submarine.

The golden metal of the hull gleams in the sun. I peer through the curved front window at the handlebar steering yoke inside. I tighten the bolts on the propeller and rudder, securing them onto the wooden rear frame.

I grab onto the front of the hull and start dragging the sub toward the water. It takes all my strength to pull it across the sand. Is it going to be too heavy to float? What if it sinks to the bottom of the ocean with me inside? I keep pulling. My legs are aching with each step, but eventually I feel the cold water of the surf lapping at my heels. I'm almost there.

With one last heave I pull the submarine out into the rolling surf.

It floats!

I open the hatch and climb inside. The sub sinks a little farther under the water with my added weight. Half the front window is sky and half is sea. This is it. I know there is no turning back from here.

What would my father say if he could see me? I think he'd be proud of what I've built . . . but he would never, ever allow me to risk my life to rescue him.

I'm sorry, Dad. I have to do this.

I close the hatch above me and dive down below the waves.

4

VISIONS

The seafloor bends downward in front of me. I pass over the ripples of sand dappled with the dancing light of the sun coming through the waves. The sand gives way to a field of smooth colorful stones. Tiny silver fish dart past my window as I glide by.

Looking up, I see the sparkling sunlight on the waves high above me. I wonder if I could make it to the surface in one breath. My hands reach out to the metal walls. They are cool to the touch, but I can't feel any water. I check the hatch above me. Everything looks dry. As long as the glass doesn't crack, the submarine is watertight.

The relief I feel at being dry rapidly disappears

when my lungs start to ache. Suddenly, the walls of the sub feel like they are getting closer. I'm breathing faster, but the air feels stale. This isn't all in my mind. *I'm running out of air*. My body is telling me to get out of the sub—now.

It's okay, I tell myself. *Don't panic. Everything is okay.*

I look up at the bottoms of the waves, far above. I try to think, but I can't focus. It hurts to breathe. The surface is far away now. I'll never make it back if I swim. My muscles are getting weak from lack of oxygen. Why didn't I think about how little air I'd have before I took the sub deep underwater?

With all my weight I push down on the right bicycle pedal at my feet. The gears rotate. I hear the propeller in the back start to turn. I pump the pedals as fast as I can. The sub is starting to move. I pull back on the handlebars, trying to steer the sub up. But I'm still sinking.

The surface looks farther and farther away. I use the last of my strength to keep pedaling. There is no more air. My muscles are too weak to move now. My body collapses onto the floor of the sub.

I see my father. He's in a tall lighthouse under the sea, its light shining through the depths.

"Keep going, Merryn," he calls to me.

The beam of the lighthouse sweeps toward my face.

The blinding light makes me squint. Why does that lighthouse look familiar? I'm sure I've seen it somewhere before.

I hear my father's voice coming from far away. He's singing a song to me. It's a melody I had long forgotten. I open my eyes. My lungs don't hurt anymore.

There is a tickle of a breeze on my ankles. Puzzled, I look down at my feet. The breeze is coming through the zephyr whelk. But how?

Now I remember the song my father was singing—it was the one about the zephyr whelk. Ancient explorers used the shells to breathe in the depths of the sea. I had always thought the stories of the explorers were just fairy tales . . . could they actually be true? Suddenly my lungs feel tight again. The sub is no longer moving, and the air from the zephyr whelk has stopped. I resume pedaling, and the breeze picks up. I think the shell must be filtering the air out of the water as the sub moves forward, just like the gills of a fish.

And just like a fish I have to keep moving in order to breathe. It seems the sub needs to stay in constant motion to filter air in. If I stop pedaling for more than a minute, my air will run out.

I pedal slowly but steadily, heading deeper into the sea. That was a close call, but I feel more confident now. Maybe I have luck on my side. Or maybe someone is watching over me. Either way, I have a good feeling that I'm going to find my father.

5

FOREST OF LIGHT

can no longer see the surface of the water above me. The sea is an endless inky darkness. I have no concept of distance or space. Giant shadows pass slowly over one another in front of me, black gliding over darkest blue.

There are tall undulating shapes passing by me, like arms reaching out of the darkness to grab hold of me. I feel something brush against the right wall of the sub.

I lean toward the window, and as I do something leans toward me. There's a face, floating in the water. It's the face of a horse. Its eyes are a pure glowing white, and its head is sleek black with a faint green glow illuminating its edges. Maybe it's just my eyes playing tricks on me.

The head turns away and I see the silhouette of its body, outlined by that eerie green glow. The front of the creature's body looks like a galloping horse, while the rear looks like the tail of a serpent. The mane and tail look like they are made of long flowing strands of seaweed, glistening and translucent in the shimmering green glow.

Every child knows the fairy tales about kelpies: beautiful horses made of the twisting underwater plants. They lure children into the water, and then pull them down to the depths below. The stories get into our heads and make us see things in the darkness. That's all it is.

Yet I can't stop myself from following it.

The kelpie's graceful flowing tail fills me with a feeling of peace and calm. It turns its head back toward me before diving deeper down. I follow it, heading deeper into the thickening shadows.

The glow of the undulating creature is hypnotizing. Where is it going? I want to stroke its beautiful mane. I can't take my eyes off it. How can any creature be so perfect and beautiful?

It's turning back toward me now, but its eyes look different and strange. They are dark and hollow instead of white. All at once, as if a veil has been lifted from my face, I see the truth. The horse's body unravels, spreading out into long tangles of flowing kelp. The kelp is moving, stretching out, surrounding me. I feel a sudden downward tug from behind me and my body lurches forward.

I am yanked downward. I lose my grip on the handlebars as I'm flung up against the roof. Strands of kelp are wrapping around and around the sub, tightening their grip. I get back onto the seat and try to pedal, but it's too late. The propeller is jammed with kelp.

Hold still, I tell myself. *Save your oxygen.* If the sub isn't moving, the zephyr whelk isn't filtering air inside.

I try to wiggle the pedal gently. Maybe I can loosen the propeller just enough to get it moving. But with each wiggle of the pedal, the kelp tightens its grip.

My breathing is slow and careful. I have to buy myself time to think.

Maybe if I rock the sub back and forth, I can loosen the grip of the kelp enough to open the hatch just a crack. I stand up on the seat, bracing my arms against either side of the roof, and lean all my weight to the left, then to the right. The sub tilts back and forth. I keep going, left, right, left, right. I push as hard as I can against the hatch.

It still won't budge.

My lungs are aching now. My head is hurting. I can't focus.

I close my eyes, breathing as slowly as I can.

I think about my father, wondering if he would have known what to do. I'm glad he can't see me now. He won't ever know I died trying to find him.

In the darkness, my mind is playing tricks on me. The sweet smell of wild orchids fills the air. I close my eyes tighter.

I hear my mother's voice in my head. She's singing a song. It's soft and low and beautiful.

Taking shallow breaths, my voice cracking, I begin to sing along with her.

In forests deep

With tangling leaves

Where kelpies sleep

And mortals grieve

If they grasp you tight

With their tendrils long

If there is no light

Recall this song

As I sing the last notes of the song, I see glowing points of light appear all around me. Hundreds of kelp bulbs are lighting up, glowing yellow and orange. I feel the submarine jostle as the strands of kelp loosen their grip and rise up to sway gently and peacefully around me.

I push down on the pedals and feel no resistance. The propeller turns and I slowly start to move forward. The air is coming in again. The great stalks of kelp seem to bend out of my way as I sail through, as if they have decided I am a friend.

The path ahead of me is lit up with the glowing balloon-like bulbs. I watch the waving strands warily. I think this must be the particularly deadly kind of kelp known as strangleclaw. I remember my father sometimes called it *glowkelp* because of its shining bulbs. He said that if you get in trouble under the water, you can use their bulbs to breathe. Each one has enough air for one or two full breaths.

At last the stalks become sparser, and I know I'm coming to the end of the forest of light. The blackness stretches out in front of me as if daring me to enter the unknown. Now I know that there will be many challenges ahead, things I can't even imagine, but I'll be ready for them.

Sure enough, as I sail on into the deeper waters, I see two gleaming green eyes watching me from the darkness.

THE CLOCKWORK SEAHORSE

The glowing green eyes stare back at me amid glints of metallic gold. I sail closer, hardly believing what I'm seeing. It looks like a *seahorse*, but it must be bigger than I am. I take some small comfort knowing that at least this horse isn't made of kelp.

It suddenly darts straight toward me, stopping just inches in front of the window.

Its eyes are huge faceted emeralds. Its body is made of interlocking segments of polished gold and its abdomen appears to be transparent crystal, revealing hundreds of tiny moving gears inside.

It turns its head from side to side as if it's looking me over. "Who made you?" I whisper, under my breath.

As it turns, I can see that the back of its head and body are covered in exposed gears. There must be thousands of them, some so small that I can barely see them.

The seahorse's body glows from inside with a dancing white light. Bright little bursts of energy crawl like lightning along the surface and then disappear back into the clockwork gears.

But its tail looks loose—it's barely attached. Is this clockwork seahorse able to swim properly with its tail so badly damaged?

As I'm thinking all this, I realize the seahorse is looking into my eyes. I suddenly feel embarrassed that I've been staring. Although it's made of metal and gears, I can't help feeling that this peculiar creature is as alive as I am.

And I think it wants something from me.

"Hello?" I say. It just stares back at me. I feel a little silly, but I keep trying. "My name is Merryn. I'm looking for someone." It tilts its head a tiny bit, as if it is listening. "I need to find my father," I continue. It tilts its head again. Does it understand me?

My face is close to the glass. The window is

starting to fog up from my breath. I'm about to wipe it clean with my sleeve when I have an idea.

With the tip of my finger I sketch a line of waves in the fogged glass. I draw my father's boat below the waves. I point to my eyes and then to the boat. The seahorse just stares at me for a moment, then turns and swims away into the darkness.

I wipe the glass free and start to pedal forward. Soon I see a faint glow ahead of me. The seahorse is waiting for me! Is it trying to lead me somewhere? Does it know where my father is? Part of me feels that it's foolish to trust this strange mechanical creature, but I don't have any better ideas at the moment.

The seahorse is moving awkwardly. I think his tail is bothering him. He's struggling to go in a straight line. *Why am I calling a pile of metal and gears a he?* I guess it just doesn't feel right to call the seahorse an *it*.

I sail closer, beckoning him to come toward me. He swims up.

"Your tail is hurt," I say. "Will you let me fix it?" He looks at me cautiously. I don't think he trusts me yet. I reach down and find my screwdriver, holding it up for him, hoping I look like I know what I'm doing.

"Follow me," I call to him, as I sail down toward a patch of kelp on the seafloor. This is going to be a tricky maneuver, but I think I can make it work. I roll my weight back and forth in the sub until it flips all the way upside down. In one quick motion I pop open the hatch and dive out. I grab a kelp strand and tie it to the hatch, holding the sub upside down. As long as it stays in this position, the air won't be able to leak out.

The water is freezing cold. I'm going to have to make this fast.

Holding my breath, I swim toward the seahorse to examine his tail. As I reach out to touch it, a spark of energy jumps onto my hand and crawls up my arm. I feel a jolt like an electric shock. At the same time, visions flash quickly through my head.

I see a beautiful city made of gold . . . then a tall underwater lighthouse, casting its searchlight through the water . . . then a circle of stones, like an undersea graveyard . . . then another flash of light, and then the images are gone.

As strange and wondrous as the images are, I have to push them out of my mind and focus on the seahorse. I need to work quickly—I won't be able to hold my breath for very long.

The creature's tail doesn't look too bad. Two of the screws have come loose and one of the gears is misaligned. Nothing I can't fix. I snap the gear back in place, and his tail immediately begins to wiggle as if he were a happy puppy. I quickly tighten the screws and check to make sure there is no other damage, then swim back up through the bottom of the hatch.

I close the hatch behind me and roll the sub back over so I can start pedaling. I'm shivering from the cold, but when I see the seahorse swim up to me, still wiggling his tail in thanks, I know I did the right thing.

The seahorse races off ahead of me, turning back periodically to make sure I am following.

"I'm coming, I'm coming," I pant. How is he able to go so fast? I keep pedaling and steering toward the light, trying not to let him out of my sight.

He zigzags back and forth, heading deeper into the sea. His head darts left and right as if he's on the lookout for predators. I can't imagine what would want to eat a mouthful of metal, but I'm not about to stop and argue.

We approach a long fissure in the seabed. It gets deeper and wider as we sail above it. Then, after looking quickly to the left and right, the seahorse dives down into the fissure. I hesitate for a moment, and then follow him. The walls are volcanic rock, bumpy and black and covered in tiny holes. We travel deeper through the fissure until we arrive at a dead end. I immediately stop pedaling when I see the wall, but I still coast forward and bump gently into the seahorse.

"Sorry!" I wave to him, embarrassed. "No brakes!" I smile and shrug to try to explain that it was an accident. The seahorse just tilts his head and looks at me. He moves forward a little bit and lightly bumps the sub, then shakes his head up and down in a way that almost looks like laughing. If I didn't know better, I'd say he was making fun of me.

The seahorse turns back and swims toward the wall. As he does, a section of the bumpy rock changes in color. The dark brown rock fades into white spots on top of smooth gray, with a single black eye staring out from the center. *It's an octopus.* With a flick of its tentacles, it shoots upward and out of our way, revealing a tunnel that leads down into the darkness below the seafloor.

The seahorse swims into the tunnel. I hesitate for a moment, thinking of the vision I had when I touched him. Who knows what dangers may await me down there?

Trusting him, I take a deep breath and follow the seahorse down into the unknown.

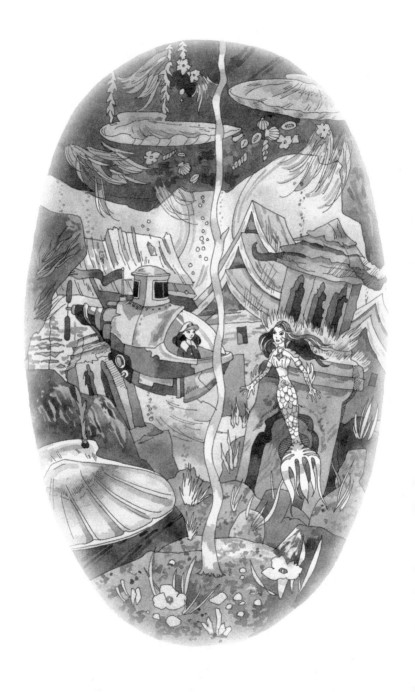

THE MERROW MAIDEN

We travel down through the rocky tunnel until it opens up into a huge undersea cavern. The cavern must be more than forty feet tall, from floor to ceiling. The walls are made of shiny black obsidian, with patches of red and orange crystal that gleam like fire opal. Rays of yellow light shine down from the ceiling, as if the sun were somehow peeking through the rock above.

Large cylindrical rock formations are grouped in clusters all around the cavern. Long strands of kelp with brightly colored bulbs grow up from the floor, stretching their flowing leaves toward the rays of light. I sail closer to the rock formations, and as I get nearer

I see why the seahorse brought me here. These aren't rock formations at all. They're houses.

This is an underwater village. Each building is round and is built from perfectly interlocking gray stones of all different shapes and sizes. The roofs are covered in shiny overlapping tiles, like beautiful gleaming fish scales. Colorful coral gardens blanket the seabed between the buildings. I can't believe what I'm seeing. Does someone *live* here? I sail from house to house, checking the windows. They are all dark and still. The only movement comes from the schools of silvery fish weaving through the rooftops.

Looking closer, I see that many of the walls are crumbling. A few of the houses have been smashed entirely, leaving only a jagged circular foundation sticking up from the ground. The rocky floor is lined with dents and craters, some more than twelve feet across. Bits of rubble lie strewn in all directions.

This must have been a very beautiful place once, but whoever lived here is now long gone. I wonder . . . could this have been where the ancient explorers lived? I suppose they would have needed domes or some other source of air, and I don't see anything like that. Whoever lived here was born to live in the sea. Could this have been a merrow village?

I feel a rush of excitement at the possibility that merrows are real. How old are these buildings, and why would the merrows have abandoned them?

I look back at the clockwork seahorse. He's floating near the center of the village, watching me. That must be where he wanted me to go . . . but why? Am I supposed to do something there?

He senses my confusion and swims over.

"What do I do?" I ask. "Is my father here?" The seahorse lowers his head. "Am I supposed to search for clues? Can you at least give me a hint?" He looks back at me and then points his head toward a tall house on my left. I sail toward it. Its round outer wall has been broken on one side, revealing what once was a merrow home.

The inside walls are covered with bright yellow and orange seashells. A tall stalk of glowkelp grows up from the center of the floor up to the ceiling. That must have provided light for the whole house. Along the walls, at different heights, are four giant clamshells attached with ropes of kelp. Those must have been beds. *A whole family of merrows once lived here.*

I get closer. The smallest of the clamshell beds hangs just below a round window that is decorated with pink and purple stones. The wall around the bed is covered with mosaic pictures made of tiny pieces of colorful stone and seashells. Each picture depicts a different adventure. In one there is a young merrow girl with flowing black hair and shiny black eyes riding on the back of a giant serpent. In another the girl is being chased by a monstrous nine-eyed squid.

I can't stop looking at the drawings. There was once a young merrow girl living here, making pictures on her wall just like me. What happened to her? What happened to her family?

My eyes move from one picture to the next, looking for some kind of answer without even knowing the question. And then I see it.

Just above the clamshell bed is a picture of the girl playing with a golden seahorse. The seahorse has emerald eyes.

Was this why the seahorse brought me here? Did he know the merrow girl?

Suddenly I have the eerie feeling that I am being watched. I turn around, but the seahorse is nowhere in sight.

I speed the sub away from the merrow house, toward the center of the village. I shouldn't have let my guard down like that—now the seahorse is gone. Did he just abandon me here? The whole village is perfectly still and quiet. Maybe I was only imagining being watched.

Then, behind the wall of the house where I had just been, I see a flash of green and blue. I sail around the back side of the building. There is nothing there. I search all around, sailing up above the colorful shining tiled roofs. And then from the corner of my eye I see the golden glint of the seahorse. He swims up toward me and wiggles his nose.

"Is there someone else here?" I ask. "Is that why you brought me here?" He tilts his head at me and then looks back down in the direction he came from. There is something coming toward me.

It's a merrow! A merrow maiden, with flowing raven hair draping down around her body.

She swims up right in front of me. Her eyes look like big shining black jewels. Her long tail moves gracefully back and forth, gleaming like it's made of blue and green sea jewels. She reaches out to touch the sub's window. I reach out in return, placing my palm against hers, with only the glass between us.

"Why are you here?" I can hear her voice in my head without her lips even moving. I don't know what to say or how to even begin.

"I'm looking for my father. He's a fisherman. Have you seen him?" She is quiet, studying me. She's looking at me the way people do when they know your face but can't remember your name. I feel self-conscious and blurt out the next thing that comes to my mind. "Are you the girl who made the pictures in the house?" If it's her, then she must have made the pictures years ago. She looks away in silence toward the ruins. I feel embarrassed, as if I said something I shouldn't have. "Are there . . . other merrows living here?" She lowers her hand from the window and turns away. "Wait!" I say. "I'm sorry!" Now I feel even worse. A terrible thought occurs to me. Is she the only one of them left?

The clockwork seahorse moves next to her. She strokes his nose with one hand. She studies his tail for a moment. Then she looks at me. Uh-oh. Can she tell that he had been damaged? Does she think that I did it?

She puts her hand back up to the window.

"Thank you," she says. "Thank you for fixing him. He says you did very good work."

"I . . . did my best," I say, weakly. "I'm sorry he got hurt." She looks at me for a while. Maybe she's never seen a human before?

"Just once," she says. Can she hear my thoughts? I feel suddenly uncomfortable. *Don't think anything stupid*, I tell myself in my head. The merrow laughs. "You're a funny one," she says. I cover my face with my hand, feeling more foolish than ever.

She swims away from me, then turns and beckons with her hand. I follow her toward a narrow tunnel in the rocky wall behind the village. She turns back to me.

"You are trying to find your father?"

"Yes! Do you know where he is?"

"Travel west from here and you will reach Skeleton Reef."

I look at her uncertainly.

"If your father's boat is anywhere below the sea, it will be there," she says.

"Thank you," I say. There is so much more I want to ask her, if I just had more time. Yesterday I thought the merrows were just a myth. Now I have to wonder if all my father's stories might be real.

I start to wave good-bye when I see a sudden look of terror in the merrow's eyes. I turn to see a golden submarine sailing toward us. Its oblong hull is perfectly smooth, without a hatch on top. At its rear is a wide fan-like rudder and from its front it casts a sweeping light back and forth through the water, as if it's searching for something.

"*This way.* Follow me," the merrow's voice says in my head. She swims around behind the wall of the house.

But that was a submarine! I want to signal to it. Maybe whoever's inside can help me search for my father.

The merrow senses my thoughts. "You don't want to get its attention," she says. "There is no one alive inside."

* * * * * *

From the shadows of a half-crumbled wall, we watch the sleek oblong submarine glide silently past. On its roof, mounted near the front, is a long segmented mechanical arm with a three-pronged metal claw at the end. Its bright searchlight sweeps past us, casting long jagged shadows across the broken rocks that were once a home.

"What is it?" I whisper once the vessel has passed by.

"A Fomori sentinel," replies the merrow. Her voice sounds colder and distant now.

"Fomori?"

"Long ago there were human explorers who visited our world. They were like you. They respected the sea. They respected *us*."

"What happened to them?" I ask, beginning to fear the answer.

"In the beginning they were friendly. We showed them our secrets. We helped them to survive the perils of the deep. Over time they grew stronger . . ."

"They didn't do *this*, did they?" I ask, gesturing to the broken walls of the ruins around me.

"They were builders and inventors. They made whole cities beneath the waves," she continues.

"They became rich from the treasures of the sea . . . and with each year that they grew richer and more powerful, they also grew more afraid."

"Afraid of what?"

"Afraid of losing it all. Afraid of everything."

"That's why they made the sentinels?" I ask.

"The sentinels are built to plunder the sea. They are unmanned automatons that tirelessly patrol every inch of the underwater world. They sink ships to steal their treasure. They crack open the seafloor to mine the gold below. They take whatever is valuable and destroy the rest."

"Including you?" I say, my voice shaking with sorrow and shame.

"Not all the Fomori were bad. Some were kind to us. A few of them left their cities and lived among us. They learned our songs. They helped us fight against the sentinels that attacked our homes."

I think of my father's songs. Could they have come from the merrows?

"Are you . . . you're not the last merrow, are you?" I ask. She looks past me for a moment, as if she is thinking of something far away. When she looks back, I can see her mind is on something else.

"Wait here," she says. "I have something that will help you." She swims to one of the beams of light coming from the ceiling. She reaches up to it, and the light seems to disappear. When she returns, she holds in her hand a bright yellow starfish. Light shines out of a white-hot circular patch at the center of the starfish's body. "It's a sunstar," she says, as she presses it gently onto the front of my submarine. "It will help you in your search for your father."

"I don't know how to thank you," I tell her, still amazed by the sight of the sunstar.

Before I can say another word, I see the white beam of the sentinel's searchlight sweep over us.

"Go!" The merrow's voice resounds in my head. I turn to see the Fomori sentinel facing us, less than twenty feet away. Its long claw arm snaps down at the merrow, narrowly missing her tail as she dodges out of the way. Three circular green emeralds form a triangle along the front face of the sentinel. *Are those what it uses to see?* The faceted emeralds look just like the eyes of the clockwork seahorse. Did the Fomori create it as well?

As these thoughts race through my mind, the sentinel turns to face me. I can see two dark hollow tubes mounted on its lower hull. I manage to dodge to my right just as a spray of bubbles appears in one of the tubes and a torpedo whizzes by me on my left.

There is a terrible cracking sound from behind me, followed by a powerful wave that sends me tumbling sideways and banging against a stone wall. Pieces of rock shower down all around me, debris from the crater left by the torpedo.

Turning back toward the source of the shot, I see the sentinel sailing over the broken walls of the village ruins. It's not looking for me. It's trying to kill the merrow.

I crank the pedals as fast as they will go and aim my sub toward the sentinel. I sail straight for it, gaining momentum as I go. At the last moment, I turn sharply, slamming into its rear propeller with the side of my sub. There is a loud clanging sound. For a moment I think I may have ruptured the wall of my own sub. I can only hope I managed to do some damage to the sentinel too.

The sentinel turns back toward me. At least I've distracted it for a moment! I turn around, trying to lead it farther away from the merrow. Across the cavern I can see the faint outline of the tunnel where I came in. I know there's no way to make it there in time, but I'm going to try anyway.

I charge full speed toward the roof, trying to get some separation from the sentinel. When I hear the burst of bubbles behind me, I dive the sub down. The torpedo slams into the ceiling above me, sending chunks of rock showering down on the roof of my sub. I keep diving down toward the floor, hoping it can't hit a moving target.

I hear another torpedo launch, closer behind me this time. I yank the controls back and the sub lurches upward as the torpedo sails underneath me and slams into the cavern wall right below the tunnel exit. I sail into the cloud of debris, unable to see where I'm going. I brace myself for the shattering of glass and the cold rush of water, but I pass through the cloud and safely into the tunnel.

I navigate up through the tunnel, pedaling so fast that my legs are burning. I see the blue water at the end of the passage up ahead as I hear another torpedo launch behind me.

8

SWISH

I race up out of the tunnel and lean into a roll, spinning the sub upside down and out of the way as the torpedo flies past me toward the distant surface of the water. Now I just need to find a place to hide before the sentinel emerges from the tunnel.

Sailing up out of the fissure, I turn toward the west and follow the seafloor, looking for a cluster of rocks, or a coral shelf, or anything at all that might conceal me. I speed across the flat sandy ground, listening for the sound of a torpedo launching behind me. The sentinel can surely outrun me in open water. My only advantage is the small head start I got when I exited the fissure.

Suddenly the seafloor disappears below me and I find myself sailing over a black bottomless trench. The darkness seems to reach up all around me, trying to swallow me whole.

I have only seconds to choose between the certain death that lies behind me and the possible death that lies beneath me.

I dive down into the depths.

Gliding deeper into the murky void, I can no longer see the mouth of the trench above me. My sunstar's light shines into the blackness of the trench, revealing nothing but empty water in all directions. But as long as I can't see the top of the trench, the sentinel shouldn't be able to see me.

I sail back and forth in a tiny pattern, just keeping the air flowing while I wait. I wonder how long I should stay down here. For all I know, the sentinel is just waiting for me up there.

Then I see something rising up from below me, a deeper darkness within the darkness. It's so big that I can't see where it starts and where it stops. The water swells up, knocking me back in the wake of the massive moving shadow.

I catch a glimpse of what look like giant green scales before I am knocked back again by another swell of water. The immense shadow disappears back into the trench, leaving me all alone, staring wide-eyed into the darkness.

Whatever that was, I don't want to wait for it to come back. I sail back up to the top of the trench. There is no sign of the sentinel in any direction. Checking my compass, I turn back to the west in search of Skeleton Reef.

I sail through the endless open sea, the sunstar casting a cone of light in front of me.

The seabed is sandy and featureless, and I feel as if I have been pedaling for hours. I check my compass to make sure I am still traveling west and not merely going in circles.

Up ahead a faint twinkling light appears in the darkness. As I sail closer, more and more tiny lights come into view. Soon there are hundreds of them, spread across the darkness like stars in the night sky.

The lights are lavender-colored, bobbing gently up and down. I can see long flowing tendrils waving beneath them. *Lantern jellies!* My father told me about them once. They are the most beautiful creatures in the sea—but they are deadly to the touch.

The bloom of jellies heads toward me. It's too late to turn around, so I hold perfectly still and let them glide by. The flickering lights cast patterns on the inner walls of the sub as they pass. Their glowing bodies are so densely packed together, I can no longer see the water at all; but they part in front of me, avoiding the light of the sunstar. I hold my breath as the long tentacles of an especially large jelly sweep over the glass in front of my face.

The jellies are becoming sparser now. The last of the glowing lights passes by me. The lavender glow recedes and I am once again sailing into the empty midnight blue.

I'm checking my compass again when I hear a sudden *whoosh* of bubbles from behind me. My mind races. The sentinel is back! *There's nowhere to hide . . . I have to outmaneuver it.*

I pull back hard on the handlebars, turning sharply to the right as I accelerate to spin into a corkscrew loop. I'm about to turn into the next loop when I feel a bump from behind me and I go spinning around again in the darkness, losing my grip on the handlebars. As I struggle to regain my balance, I see two giant yellow eyes staring at me through the window.

It's not the sentinel. It's a serpent—*a baby leviathan*.

Its long green snake-like body flows gracefully as it watches me. My father's stories of leviathans used to give me nightmares, but this one doesn't look *too* terrifying. I wonder . . . could that giant shadowy creature I saw in the trench have been a full-grown leviathan?

"Hi there," I say. He just stares at me, his long body undulating behind him. "Are you lost? Your mother is probably worried about you. Maybe you should go find her." He touches his nose against the window. He's actually kind of cute, in a weird sort of way.

"Really, I mean it. If she sees you here, she's going to be mad at me." I turn and try to sail around him, but he just swims alongside me and gets in front of me again. This time he swishes his tail back and forth as if he wants to play.

"Listen, I wish I could play, but I'm in a hurry." He just swishes his tail again.

He taps my front window with a fin and then turns and swims off ahead of me, stopping to turn his head back to see if I'm following. Is he trying to play tag?

Well, he's going in the same direction I am . . . I guess it doesn't hurt to have a fierce-looking traveling companion.

When he sees that I'm following him, he swishes his tail even faster and darts forward into the darkness. I guess we're playing tag after all. I don't know why, but I suddenly feel happier. For the first time since I started out, I feel like I'm not alone on my journey.

The little leviathan does a looping corkscrew turn in front of me. Is he imitating what I was trying to do earlier? I can't help laughing. He's such a little show-off. He turns back toward me as if he wants my approval. He swishes his tail playfully, waiting for me to catch up.

Swish. I'm going to call him Swish.

*   *   *   *   *   *

With Swish swimming along at my side, I sail past the steep rocky edge of the trench. It feels good to see sand below me again. Swish suddenly races off, chasing something. He disappears into the darkness for a moment, then races back toward me. Only then do I realize what he's chasing. It's a fifteen-foot-long thresher shark.

I turn to get out of their path and the long-tailed shark speeds past me. Swish stops chasing him and returns to swimming alongside me. Until now I hadn't realized just how big Swish is. The shark was barely half his size.

"I'm glad you're on my side," I say to Swish. The thresher shark probably wouldn't have tried to attack the sub, but it feels good knowing that Swish is trying to protect me.

Swish swims down along the seafloor, wriggling his long body back and forth in the sand and making a snaking pattern behind him. He turns around and looks at his creation, then at me. I think he wants me to do the same thing.

I glide downward, letting the sub graze against the sand, and zigzag back and forth, trying to make a trail. Swish slides along beside me as I go. I turn back around to look at the patterns. My trail looks like a creek alongside a huge riverbed, but Swish wags his tail excitedly as he races around in circles above our art display.

"Come on, now," I tell him, laughing at his antics. "We have important responsibilities." We turn back to the west and he swims alongside me again. I think he understands that we're going somewhere.

Swish alternates between swimming by my side and scouting ahead of me, looking for dangers to protect me from. In front of me, he stops suddenly, staring straight ahead.

"What is it this time, a deadly puffer fish?" I joke.

Then I see what he's looking at. There are thirteen tall rectangular stones sticking up out of the sand, forming the shape of a circle. Each stone must be at least twelve feet high. This couldn't have been a natural formation. I get a strange eerie feeling as I look at the circle of stones. I wonder if this is an old merrow graveyard.

Swish is staring into the center of the circle. He slowly backs away from the stones as if he is scared of something.

"They're just rocks," I say to him, as I sail between two stones and into the center of the circle. He makes a yelping noise and thrashes his tail. "It's okay; I'm fine!" I say to him as he swims around the outside of the circle anxiously.

And then I hear it. There is *music* all around me.

It sounds like the voices of men and women singing together. There are no words, just a low and sad melody. I look around to see where the sound is coming from, but it seems to be all around me. Without thinking, I hum along to the tune. It feels strangely familiar. Was this one of my father's lullabies?

Swish is getting more and more anxious, but I can't leave the circle. I can feel that there's something here. This is where I need to be.

The music moves through me. It becomes a part of me. The song feels so familiar, but I can't place it. I don't think it's one of my father's lullabies. Wait . . . I remember now . . .

This was the same song my mother sang to me on the day she died.

The world seems to fall away beneath me.

I'm in a rowboat with my mother. I see our house in the distance, across the water. My father is on the beach waving to us. My mother is wearing a green dress and a necklace of wild orchids. She is humming a beautiful sweet melody.

"What's that song?" I ask.

"It's something my mother used to sing to me," she answers.

"Why are there no words in that one?"

"Good question. Maybe its meaning is different for every person."

"What does it mean to you?"

"To me, it means to always cherish and remember those who you love."

I look down at my own wild orchid necklace, then back up at my mother's dark brown hair shining in the sun. Her beautiful green eyes twinkle as she smiles at me.

"Do you think we'll see a whale today?" I ask.

"I'm sure we will. They love the scent of wild orchids. They come up to the surface just to smell them."

"Whoa . . ." I say, peering over the side, looking for a whale. "Do you think I can ride one?"

"Of course," she says with a laugh. "It's Sunday, so they shouldn't be too busy."

"I think I see one!" I shout, leaning farther over the edge. There's a dark shadow moving deep beneath the surface.

"Careful," she says, as she reaches for my hand. But it's too late.

As I lean out to touch the water, I tumble down into the sea. My arms and legs are flailing as I sink below the surface. I kick at the water, helplessly trying to reach for the boat edge. The shadow of the boat shrinks against the sunlit water. Strands of kelp reach up around me as my feet are pulled down to the ground.

There is a splash above me. My mother comes toward me, her arm reaching out.

I feel the kelp tighten around my legs. She swims down and pulls my arm, trying to free me from the grip of the kelp. I can't keep my mouth closed anymore.

I see that my mother's eyes are filled with fear. She frantically pulls the kelp away from my legs and lifts me up. She pushes me up toward the sunlight above us.

I flail my arms.

I kick as hard as I can.

My mother's hand lets go of me. She reaches out, trying to push me toward the surface. But now the kelp has grabbed hold of her.

I can't hold my breath any longer. My mouth opens up and the water flows in. The water is in my lungs. I'm sinking again. I close my eyes. Everything feels cold.

Then something grabs me and pulls me up. I'm coughing. I can't stop coughing. I'm on the boat. I'm breathing again. My father is staring at me, anxiously.

There's a splash again, and he's back in the water. He's gone a long time. When he comes back, he has my mother in his arms. She's in the boat. He's trying to make her breathe.

I reach for her hand. Her eyes are open, but she's not looking at me. Her orchid necklace has come off. I want to tell her I'll make her a new one. I want to tell her I'm sorry. My father keeps trying to make her breathe. But she's not breathing. I squeeze her hand as tight as I can. And the world falls away from me again.

I'm back in the middle of the circle of stones. The sad melody is all around me. *It was my fault.*

She died trying to save me. That's why I had forgotten that day. That's why my father never talks about it. Does he blame me for it too? Does he feel guilty that he saved me and couldn't save her? I shudder as I think of how my father would feel if he ever learned that I died while trying to save him.

I sit and listen to the sweet peaceful sound of the notes. My eyelids start to feel heavy.

The air is hard to breathe, but I don't have the energy to move anymore. I see Swish, still swimming around outside the circle. He'll be okay. He can go back to his mother. I just want to stay here. All I want is to listen to the sad lullaby of the stones, just a little while longer . . .

I feel my whole body getting heavy. I'm just going to lie down for a little while. I curl up on the cold metal floor of my sub and listen to the song all around me as everything starts to go dark.

A sudden jolt startles me, as the sub is yanked backward. I look up out the window to see a cloud of sand, then the stones retreating in the distance.

The music is gone. I feel as if I'm waking up. Instinctively, I start to pedal. Swish's face pops up in front of me, his eyes wide with worry. He must have pulled me out of the circle. He saved my life.

The air is coming back again. I look out at Swish swimming beside me.

"I wish I could hug you," I say.

Somehow I think he understands.

9

SKELETON REEF

S wish and I continue to sail west. He seems to be enjoying the adventure, but part of me fears that he may turn around and leave at any moment. After all, he doesn't know where we are going or why. To him this probably just feels like some sort of game. Or is it possible that he can sense the truth? Maybe he wants to help me get safely to my destination.

In the distance I can see huge jagged shadows jutting up above the horizon.

"Is that Skeleton Reef?" I ask Swish. He senses the excitement on my face and races off in front of me to scout ahead. I stare out at the sharply angled shadows in the distance, wondering how the reef earned its name.

As we sail closer, I feel a knot in my stomach. I'm excited by the hope of finding my father and at the same time I'm frightened of what I might find instead. I remind myself over and over: If I can survive this long below the waves, so can he.

Swish is swimming in circles, chasing a school of silvery fish. The fish group into a ball, exploding apart as Swish dives through the center, then balling up again after he passes by.

"Let's go, Swish. Leave the poor fish alone," I call to him. And then, in a flash, the fish disappear down through the seafloor, and Swish dives down after them, vanishing before my eyes.

I sail up to the spot where he disappeared. At first it seems that he just dove straight down into the sand of the seafloor, but as I look closer I see that there's a thin layer of sand covering what looks like a sheet of fabric. Only it's not fabric . . . it's webbing. It's a trapdoor entrance covered with a thick spiderweb.

"Come on, Swish. Come out," I plead.

There is no sound from the trapdoor. I wait, expecting Swish to pop back out at any second. I look toward the shadows of Skeleton Reef, then back to the camouflaged webbing. I know I can't just leave Swish down there.

I gather speed and dive through the web.

It's nearly pitch black down below. As my eyes adjust to the darkness, I see faint glows of spiny blue moon urchins along the walls. I'm inside some kind of cave. I sweep my sunstar's light through the cloudy water, looking for any sign of Swish. The walls are covered in what looks like layers upon layers of spiderwebs.

I sweep my light downward and let out a scream at what it illuminates. The bottom of the cave is covered from wall to wall in a giant web. At the center of the web is an impossibly big black spider. Its body must be more than ten feet across. Long segmented black legs are tumbling a thick webbed cocoon around with a flurry of precise movements.

I am frozen with fear as I stare down at the hideous creature. My breath is coming in short ragged gasps. I've never liked spiders. Even little ones scare me. My arms go rigid and my hands tremble uncontrollably.

I remember an old story of my father's, about the Watcher. He only ever told it once, years ago—it scared me so much that he never brought it up again. He said the Watcher is a giant diving bell spider that feeds on creatures of the deep. A shiny bubble of air around its abdomen allows it to breathe as it waits beneath the seafloor, devouring any unsuspecting soul that enters its lair. It has lived for ages, my father said, and will likely live for ages more.

I stare down at it in horror, wondering how many living things have met their end here.

The Watcher stops wrapping the cocoon and turns its head up toward me, its eight black eyes shining in the ray of light from my submarine. The cocoon wiggles back and forth, and through a small gap in the webbing I can see a patch of green scales. It's Swish!

I forget my fear. Without even thinking, I flip the sub over, pop out of the hatch, and swim toward the giant spider. In a flash, it releases the cocoon and grabs me by the waist, pulling me toward its mouth. Its sharp black fangs are closing down on me. I grab onto one of the fangs with both hands and twist it sideways with all my strength. It snaps in half. The

Watcher loosens its grip just enough for me to slip out of its claws and swim down underneath its belly.

I pull the coral knife from my belt and thrust it as hard as I can into the glistening bubble of air around the Watcher's abdomen. The bubble bursts like a giant balloon, sending thousands of smaller bubbles rushing up toward the ceiling of the cave. The Watcher frantically flails its legs, trying to move toward the surface, but its heavy body sinks down into its own web. It writhes in the web, becoming more tangled as it thrashes.

I swim to the cocoon, cutting it free and releasing Swish. He darts up out of the silk webbing and out of sight, above me.

I slide back through the sub's hatch, taking a huge, relieved breath of air. A little bit of water got into the sub when I went out, but it's not too bad. I sail back up out of the cave, and Swish is waiting there for me.

My heart is still pounding in my chest as I look at Swish. He's waggling his tail back and forth hesitantly. He thinks I'm mad at him.

"Come on, boy." I smile.

He swims close by my side toward the jagged shadows of Skeleton Reef.

* * * * * *

The shadows on the horizon grow larger and more distinct. I'm starting to see individual shapes within them. Tall thin shadows stick up out of larger ghostly black masses. If that's a reef up ahead, it's unlike any I've ever seen before.

I look at Swish, realizing what we are seeing.

"It's a graveyard of ships," I whisper. The tangled wreckage stretches on as far as I can see. Broken hulls and battered masts are piled on top of one another in all directions. All different sizes and types of ships lie jumbled together on the seafloor.

I sail over the barnacle-encrusted remains of an old wooden freighter. Could the Fomori sentinels have done this? Or did something else bring these ships down? I recall the dream I had of the great tentacle arm pulling my father's boat underneath the waves.

I drift over the hills of wreckage, searching for any sign of my father's tiny boat.

In the distance I see the sweeping lights of Fomori sentinels. They must be searching the wreckage too. One of them sails toward me, its light still aimed downward at the wreckage below.

I turn toward Swish and hold my finger to my lips. As long as we stay away from the searchlight, I don't think it will notice us. I watch as its thin metal arm reaches into the wreckage of a ship. The claw snaps up an old wooden shipping crate, crushing it into pieces. The sentinel must be looking for valuables in the wreckage.

I carefully follow along behind the gliding vessel. If my father's boat is down here, the sentinel might lead me to it. Swish swims alongside me, glancing toward me protectively every few seconds.

Then I see it.

My father's boat is pointing nosedown in the wreckage, a gaping hole in its port bow. The sentinel reaches its claw arm inside the boat, but it comes back empty. I watch its searchlight pass over the boat and into the darkness beyond.

Checking that there are no other sentinels nearby, I flip the sub over once again and swim out the hatch and down to the boat. I squeeze in through the hole in the bow and swim inside. There's a pocket of air trapped at the back. I swim up into it and take a breath. The faint light from my sub shines in through a porthole window.

My father isn't here. But he must have had air, at least for a little while.

I look around the hollow hull of the boat, hoping to find some clue about what happened to him. Then I see something wedged between two boards—his journal.

The journal is a little wet, but I can still read what's on the pages. It's filled with my father's notes about fish migration patterns. He's drawn maps showing his routes at sea. He's sketched a little fish at the locations where he was successful, and an X in the places where there were no fish. As I flip through the pages, I see that there are fewer and fewer locations marked with a fish. By the end of the journal, the maps are completely covered with Xs.

I flip past the last page and see my father has written a note. *It's written to me.*

Did he write this after the boat sank? My heart races as I read it:

My dearest Merryn,

I fear I may never see you again. As I write this, I am far beneath the sea, brought down by a creature I cannot even describe.

If my boat is one day salvaged and these words should find you, I hope you will stay strong in my absence. Please know I wanted nothing more than to return home.

I'm sorry I'm not there for you now. I'm sorry I didn't provide you a better life. It pains me to think of all the times you went hungry without saying a word. I wish I could have given you pretty dresses and books and paints. You deserve so much better than what I was able to give.

I am going to take a deep breath and try to make it to the surface.

I love you more than all the world,

Dad

I close my eyes as tightly as I can. Tears roll down my cheeks. I don't want pretty dresses or paints. All I want is to open my eyes and see my father again.

My eyes open slowly. I'm alone in the darkness.

I tuck the journal under my arm and swim back out of the boat and through my submarine's hatch. My father didn't give up. He was trying to reach the surface. I look at the darkness of the water above me. How far is it to the surface? Could he have made it?

Swish peers in at me through the window. He knows I'm sad and doesn't know what to do.

"It's okay, Swish. We're not giving up. We're going to find him." I put my hand up to the window. He rubs his head against the glass next to my hand.

My eyes refocus toward the distance as an enormous silhouette glides over the jagged wreckage. Long flowing tentacles trail behind the fast-moving shadow. The searchlights of the Fomori sentinels turn and follow the shadow eastward out of the reef.

Could that be the creature that is sinking the ships? The sentinels followed it, but they didn't attack. Maybe they are tracking it. Or maybe it's the other way around—is it possible that creature is actually the one controlling the sentinels?

A voice from behind me startles me out of my musings.

"I see you've made a friend." The merrow maiden swims up to my window and strokes Swish's head. He wiggles his tail happily. She turns back toward me. "Did you find your father's boat?"

"Yes, but he's gone."

"Good," she says. When she sees the hurt look on my face, she adds, "There wouldn't have been enough air for him to survive. If he's not in the boat, then there's hope that he's okay."

"Oh," I say, embarrassed that I misunderstood her intent. "But how do I find him now?"

"There is a strong current that runs through the reef. It was once used by the early Fomori explorers. It passes directly above us. If your father tried to make it to the surface, he may have been caught in it."

"Where does it lead?"

"Somewhere I cannot go, I'm afraid." I think this over, uneasy at the thought of using a Fomori pathway alone. "Follow me and I'll show you the current," says the merrow as she swims up above the wreckage.

"Do you know what sunk these ships?" I ask. She doesn't seem to hear me. Or maybe that's a conversation we don't have time for right now.

"Here is the current," she says, pointing to a powerful flow of water that courses, nearly invisibly, through the wreckage of the reef. "You should hurry. I will tell you all you want to know the next time we meet."

I see the light of a Fomori sentinel approaching us. I hesitate. If it sees me enter the current it will be able to follow me, and I may have no way to escape. But the merrow is already one step ahead of me.

"You have to go," she says firmly. She swims toward the sentinel's light, distracting it away from me. I see it turn toward her as she dives into the wreckage to hide. I wait a moment longer, unsure what to do.

It's now or never. I sail into the current.

I feel a sudden, powerful tug and the world around me becomes a blur.

10

THE DEEPLIGHT

The wreckage of Skeleton Reef flies by me on either side as the current pulls me down past the twisted remains of ships and along a winding sandy riverbed. It's useless to pedal. The current is too powerful for me to break free. Wherever it's taking me, I'm now at its mercy.

I pass beyond Skeleton Reef, back into open water. In the distance, across a long stretch of rolling sand, I see the shadow of a tall tower. A powerful beam of light shines from the top of the tower. *It's the undersea lighthouse.*

As we near the tower, the current speeds up, and I'm pulled into the darkness as it yanks me down into a tunnel below the sandy floor. Then, just as abruptly,

I feel myself being tugged upward. At last there is a lurching jolt and my submarine comes to rest.

I'm bobbing in the water. Half my window is light and half is dark.

I lift open the hatch, scarcely believing what I'm seeing. The sub is floating *above* the water. I'm inside the tower, in a wide circular pool at the center of a huge stone room. Tall gray walls of stone rise up, forming a cold cylindrical prison. I jump out of the hatch and splash down in the water.

A moment later, Swish pops his head up right next to me. He must have followed me in the current.

I swim to the edge of the pool and lift myself out onto the stone floor. My legs feel unsteady. This is the first time I have been able to stand up in hours.

"I'm going to go look around," I call to Swish. "I'll be right back, okay?" He wags his tail in the water as if to say *yes*, but I can tell from his eyes that he's worried about me.

I look around the big round room. A narrow stone staircase curves along the interior wall of the huge cylindrical tower, disappearing through a hole in the ceiling high above me.

As I walk over to the base of the steps, I see something black lying on the floor. It's a glove. Not just any glove, but a heavy rubber fishing glove with a faded picture of a dandelion painted on the back. *It's my father's glove.*

My father was here. Maybe he still *is* here, somewhere in this tower. He must have followed the current, just like the merrow said. I pick up the glove. It has a large tear in it that runs from the front of the wrist to the middle of the hand. Did it snag on something in the fast journey through the current? Or was he attacked by something? Despite my new fears, this is the first evidence I've found to suggest my father might still be alive.

I feel a rush of happiness and hope as I race up the stairs and through a hole in the ceiling. I emerge onto the floor above and find twelve beds, each with neatly folded white sheets, arranged in a ring around the perimeter of the circular room. In the middle of the room are three square wooden tables, each with four chairs. At the very center of the room, in between the tables, is a glass column that runs all the way up into the ceiling. The circular stone wall that surrounds the room is embedded with four glass hemispheres, all taller than doors and reinforced with strips of rusted iron. They each face one of the cardinal directions: north, east, south, and west. Three of the glass cases are empty, but inside the fourth is a ball-shaped submersible, the top half made of glass and the bottom made of gold. It's just big enough for a person to fit inside. Attached to the wall adjacent to the glass hemisphere, there is a lever. *Is this how they transport people in and out of the tower?*

I look inside at the last remaining submersible. The front of its glass top has been smashed, as if the vessel met with some violent collision. Behind the broken glass, I can't see any form of steering controls or navigation. Each of the submersibles must be designed to go to a specific location all on its own.

I return to the center of the room and study the tall glass tube that rises to the ceiling. On one side there is an oval opening big enough for me to step into an oblong golden capsule. Judging from what I've seen of the Fomori's creations so far, this must be some means of transportation. But where is it going to go? I step in, nervously, and immediately a flap seals the tube shut and I hear a rush of air as I am yanked upward. I zip through the ceiling and into darkness. For a moment I feel weightless, and then the capsule bounces slightly and I come to a stop. I step into a tall round room with windows that go from the floor to the ceiling.

Beyond the walls of glass, the sea stretches out below me in all directions. I must be in the top of the tower. At the center of the room, near the ceiling, there is a powerful white light housed in a hemisphere of gleaming gold. It rotates slowly, sweeping its beam out through the windows and deep into the sea. Below it is a contraption made of heavy gears and exposed levers, all steadily turning, keeping the light in constant motion. I watch the sweeping white beam piercing through the empty blue water outside.

As I follow the light with my eyes, I hear my mother's voice. A long-forgotten memory is suddenly vivid in my mind. I can see myself lying in my bed under a patchwork blanket. The distant sound of crashing waves rises up through my window. My mother is sitting at the edge of my bed, telling me a story.

"Deep beneath the sea, in the darkest depths, there is a tall tower, made of stone. And atop the tower is a shining beacon of light," she says. She looks down sadly as she speaks. "They call this tower the Deeplight."

"Is it a lighthouse?" I ask.

"Yes, in a way it is."

"But how can there be ships under the sea?"

"The light isn't there to help guide ships. It's there to search for things."

"Like what?"

She is quiet for a moment. "You know how some of the things under the sea are scary?"

"Like leviathans?"

"Yes, like leviathans. The tower was built to keep people safe against the scary things," she explains. "But sometimes . . ." She stops, as if the rest is hard for her to say.

"Sometimes what?"

"Sometimes things don't work out the way they were supposed to. Sometimes people are scared of things . . . even though they shouldn't be." Her eyes appear to look far away. I wonder what she's thinking.

"Did something bad happen at the lighthouse?"

"Yes, I'm afraid so. But that part of the story will have to wait."

"Until tomorrow?"

"Until you are this tall," she says, smiling now as she holds her hand a few inches above my head.

"Promise?" I ask.

"Promise." She kisses my forehead.

I shiver as the memory fades away and I am back in the cold stone room. *The Deeplight*. It's strange to think that I am actually standing inside it. I wonder what could have happened here that was so terrible. Why did my mother not want to tell me?

I look around at the windows that surround the circular room. Chairs are mounted into the floor, facing toward the windows, and in front of each chair are what look like metal handlebars, except the handles are pointed upward. Peering out the window, I can see a ballista poking out from the tower below the window. Its heavy barbed-iron spear is aimed and ready to launch out into the water. And that's when I realize: This isn't a lighthouse at all. These are turrets. This is a fortress.

I think about how the merrow said she never comes near the tower. This tower must have been built by the Fomori to battle the merrows. I watch the searchlight sweeping its slow arc through the depths. In the distance I see the gleam of a golden sentinel. Is the tower still helping the sentinels find the merrows, even now?

Then I remember why I entered the Deeplight in the first place, and I am jolted by a terrible thought: *I am at the top of the tower, and my father isn't here.* Where could he have gone? The only possibility I can think of is that he took one of the submersibles from the room below. But the only one of them that remains is broken, so I have no way to follow him.

I wonder if the merrow maiden knows where the submersibles go. Where is she now? I think of how she lured the sentinel away from me to allow me to make it safely to the Deeplight. She risked her life to help me reach a tower that was used to hunt her own people . . . Why would she do that?

My mother knew the truth about the Deeplight. Her voice was so certain, she must have known it was more than just a story. Had she actually seen it before? I remember the sadness in her eyes when she spoke of it. Up above me, the immense powerful light shines out into the sea. I think of all the merrows who must have died because of this light. I can't let that go on any longer.

I hope my mother would be proud of me for what I am about to do.

I leap up and grab onto the lip above the entrance to the glass chute. Lifting my leg up over it, I grab onto one of the levers that is part of the moving machinery turning the light. I pull myself up until I can see the complex inner workings that drive it. I stare at the moving parts in awe, thinking of how long these hundreds of gears have been turning on their own without anyone to repair them. This is truly a masterwork of engineering, unlike anything I have ever seen.

And now I am going to destroy it.

The bolts along the base of the frame come loose with a few hard twists. Holding on to one of the slow-moving levers, I pull myself along the edge of the frame, loosening each bolt as I go. I can feel the whole frame begin to wobble as I turn the last bolt. I give it one big push and leap down to the ground.

The frame topples over, pulling the enormous light down with it. I cover my face as the light shatters into a million shards that spray across the room in all directions. A thunderous clanging of metal echoes through the room as the heavy gears smash apart and roll toward the walls.

The sea outside the windows is dark now. The Deeplight is no more.

A little shard of glass is stuck in my left hand. I pull it out carefully and put pressure on the cut to stop the bleeding. It doesn't look too deep. Looking at the long knife-like slivers of glass across the floor, I realize how lucky I am not to have been more badly hurt.

Out of the corner of my eye there is a tiny golden glow. I turn toward the window and see the clockwork seahorse staring in at me from the water outside. How did he find me here? Did the merrow send him?

He swims up to the window and taps it with his nose a few times. Then he looks at me.

"Yes, it's nice to see you too," I say. He tilts his

head at me as if he is trying to tell me something, then swims forward and taps the glass again. He's tapping in a kind of pattern. I tap the pattern back on the glass: five taps . . . one tap . . . five taps.

He leans forward and points down with his nose.

"You want me to go down? Down where?" I ask. He taps the glass again in the same pattern, then points down. He looks back up at me to see if I understand. "Okay," I say, nodding to him. I still don't know what he's saying, but the best I can do is go down to the lower level and try to figure it out.

I get back in the glass chute, and it zips me down to the room below. Did the seahorse want me to take a submersible? I think of the pattern of taps: five, one, five. Or was he just tapping out the number eleven? I look at the twelve beds, arranged in a ring around the room. Is there something special about the eleventh bed? How would I even know which one is the eleventh? They're in a circle—there's no beginning!

A plaintive howling sound rings out, and I remember that I left Swish all alone. I race down the steps into the room below. Swish splashes his tail in the water excitedly as he sees me.

"I'm sorry, Swish! I didn't mean to take so long," I tell him, rubbing his head. He rolls over in the water, ready to go play. With another splash of his tail, he dives down into the deep circular pool and out of sight. Could the seahorse have wanted me to find something in the pool?

I step back into the submarine and dive down below the surface. Swish circles around me, ready to start a new game of tag.

"Hold on, boy, I just need to look for something," I tell him as he eagerly swims up to my window and then darts away. The pool is much deeper than I first realized, and there are tunnels leading out from it at varying depths. Some of the tunnels have water flowing out of them and into the pool, while others have water flowing in.

I think this place must be a nexus of underground currents. The Fomori would have used these tunnels to travel to all different parts of the sea. Above each tunnel there are symbols etched into the stone—of stars, triangles, and vertical lines. Was the seahorse telling me which tunnel to take?

One tunnel has three lines, followed by a triangle.

Another has a star and two lines. The seahorse tapped eleven times, so I look for two vertical lines.

Swish swims back up to me, wondering why I am staring at the walls instead of playing with him.

"Do you want to race me?" I ask him, nodding and putting on an excited smile. He swishes his tail back and forth. "I'm going to go through a tunnel, and I want you to follow me, okay?" His whole body is wiggling in anticipation. He might not understand me, but he knows we're about to do something fun.

I look back at the tunnels, remembering the seahorse's pattern of taps: five, one, five. What if the five taps represented a five-sided star? I search the tunnels, one by one, until I see one with a star, a vertical line, and another star. There is a powerful current flowing into it. This has to be the right one.

"Ready, Swish?" I call out as I sail toward the gaping circular mouth. Then I'm pulled in more suddenly than I expected. "Ahhh!" I scream in shock as the current whips me into the tunnel at lightning speed.

11

THE SEAGARDEN

The gray stone walls of the tunnel fly by in a
seemingly unending blur. I brace my arms against
the walls of the sub as it bangs back and forth
against the hard stone. My stomach lurches with each
new turn, and I half expect to be thrown through the
glass window at any moment. I hear the sound of
rushing water getting louder and higher pitched. The
tunnel narrows.

Then, with a sudden heaving jolt, I am launched up
out of the tunnel and into a world of color.

I am surrounded by a garden of a thousand different
hues. My eyes go wide. In all my dreams of the sea, I
never imagined anything as beautiful as this. Purple

blooms of acropora stretch out their fuzzy fingers like spring lilacs. Orange sun polyps blossom in great dazzling bouquets. Red carnation corals shoot out like flames. Bundles of translucent blue bubble coral shimmer in rays of gleaming light. And everywhere I look there are schools of fish, swooping up and down in great undulating patterns like flocks of starlings. The whole garden is alive with movement.

Something bumps me from below, and I see Swish's head pop up in front of my window. He swims a slow wide circle, taking in the sights around us. I can tell from his reaction that he's never seen anything like this either.

I sail over the brightly colored coral, exploring this newfound wonder. A graceful stone-shelled kelp turtle turns its head toward me as I pass, its rocky shell broader than my submarine. It feels so peaceful here. This place looks like it has never been touched by the Fomori.

A familiar glint of gold emerges from a clump of waving sea grass and comes toward me. The clockwork seahorse floats just in front of me, beckoning with his head for me to follow.

He swims down to a little nook within the rocks and points toward a speck of orange peeking out from underneath a small pile of loose rocks. There's something hidden there.

I really don't want to go back into the freezing water again, but I sense that this is important. With a quick roll of the sub, I dive out of the hatch and hurry toward the nook. I brush aside the loose rocks. Underneath is a thin gold chain necklace with an orange seashell as a pendant. I look closer at the shell. It's a zephyr whelk!

Holding the shell up to my lips, I take a slow, careful breath. The air feels salty and wet, but it works. I look back at Swish and then at the seahorse to see if they share my astonishment. *I'm breathing underwater*. Bubbles tickle my nose as I laugh in spite of myself. I put the necklace on over my head, still giddy with excitement over this new discovery. As long as I don't lose the zephyr whelk, I'll never have to worry about running out of air outside the sub. The seahorse points again toward the rocks where the whelk had been.

"Thank you," I try to say to him, releasing another

mouthful of bubbles. He points back to the rocks once more. I look back and pull a few more rocks aside, revealing a piece of pale orange fabric. Pulling it out, I realize that it's an old diving suit. The fabric is soft and stretchy. The seahorse looks from the suit to me and back again.

Sure, why not, I think. I pull the suit on over my shirt and shorts. Although it looked several sizes too large when I was holding it, the fabric seems to shrink to my body. I can no longer feel the cold of the water at all; I feel as if I am in my bed, snuggled inside a warm blanket.

"How is this possible?" I ask the seahorse. I look toward Swish and shrug. He swims up to me, looking me over with curiosity. He seems as surprised as I am by my new outfit. "Now we can play tag!" I say, tapping his front fin and swimming away as fast as I can. Swish chases after me, and I dodge away as he tries to tag me back. The corals below me look like a rainbow of summer blossoms. A shiny golden glint in the sand catches my eye, and I dive down just as Swish comes racing back to tag me.

I brush off the sand, discovering the glint is a

heavy golden coin almost as big as my palm. On one side is an engraving of a tower that looks like the Deeplight, while the other side has the image of a coiled serpent. Running my hand through the sand, I find two more coins. They both show the Deeplight on one side, but they each have a different engraving on the back. One shows what looks like a gleaming golden city, and the other has a picture of a shell that looks like a zephyr whelk. I put the three coins into the pocket of my diving suit. My father will want to see these too.

As I look back up, I see the clockwork seahorse swim toward me and beckon for me to follow. I meet his eyes, looking at him sheepishly.

"I'm sorry," I say. "You brought me here for a reason, didn't you?"

He leads me across the colorful gardens of coral, down to the mouth of a small cave that lies at the base of a tall sheet of rock. I peer inside. The floor of the cave is covered in what look like glowing rubies, each one as big as the tomatoes from my garden. I follow the seahorse through the entrance and into the cave. Lying on the ground, her body curled up around the rubies, is the merrow. As I get closer, I realize that these aren't rubies at all—they're eggs.

The merrow seems to be sleeping. I swim closer, careful not to wake her, and in the faint glow of light from the eggs I can see her face is pale. There is a long gash in her tail as well as a red cloud in the water above it. She must have been hurt by the sentinel back at Skeleton Reef.

"I'm so sorry," I say. "How can I help?" The seahorse just looks from the merrow to me. He brought me here in hopes that I would know what to do. I look at the merrow with a feeling of utter helplessness.

Stay calm, I tell myself. *You can do this.*

My father taught me how to bandage a wound, but I've only ever had to do it once. Even then it was only a minor cut on his arm from a jagged piece of scrap in the nets. I've never had to bandage anything serious before . . . and besides, I have no bandages to work with! I'm going to have to find some way to improvise.

I swim out of the cave and find a cluster of tall swaying kelp stalks. I take out my coral knife and cut each stalk at the base. Back in the cave, I wrap the stalks tightly around the merrow's wounded tail, tying the ends with a square knot to keep them secure.

It looks like the bleeding has stopped, but she is still pale and weak. I'm going to have to find her something to eat.

I swim along the seafloor, gently lifting up the colorful fan-like corals and searching the sand underneath. In just a few minutes, I have collected ten violet-shelled scallops. I bring them back to the merrow and open the shells with the coral knife. The merrow's eyes open halfway, but they are distant and unfocused. I hold a scallop up to her lips and she takes a tiny bite.

I keep feeding her, and, after a few minutes, she is able to sit up. She looks at the ruby-colored eggs. I can tell she is counting them in her head. There are thirty-three. I counted them twice already as I was feeding her. I look at the eggs, each glowing faintly from within, and wonder if these are the very last merrow eggs in all the sea.

"Seagarden," the merrow says, startling me as she speaks. I look at her quizzically. "We call it the

Seagarden," she says, indicating the clockwork seahorse and herself. "It lies in the shadow of a ridge in the sea that protects it from the eyes of the Deeplight. It's the last place in the sea untouched by the Fomori sentinels."

"I, uh . . . I turned off the Deeplight," I say, not wanting to explain that I had smashed it. Her eyes widen, and she is quiet for a long while.

"Thank you," she says at last. "That will help make the sea safe again." She looks toward the cave entrance, deep in thought.

"What's wrong?"

I look out the cave entrance. High above the coral, I see the sweeping light of a Fomori sentinel passing silently over us.

"With the Deeplight off," she whispers, "the sentinels have altered their patrols. Eventually one of them will find the Seagarden." She sees my horrified expression. "It's not your fault. You did a very good thing."

I peer out of the cave. The sentinel is nowhere in sight. But I know it's just a matter of time before it returns.

The merrow is still too weak to swim; and even if she could, I know she would never leave her eggs if there was any danger nearby. I need to figure out some way to stop the sentinels.

"What are they looking for?" I ask the merrow.

"Gold," she says. "Minerals, gems . . . anything the Fomori found valuable. The sentinels destroy anything in their path and dig up the seafloor to mine what they want." I think of the lifeless blue void I saw from the top of the Deeplight. Then I think of my father stepping out of his boat with empty fishing nets. How long has this been going on?

"Where do they take the gold when they find it?"

"To a place no one else can go. The Forbidden City."

"That's where the Fomori live? If I *did* get there somehow, could I stop the sentinels?"

"Even if you could stop them, there is something worse." There is a tremble in her voice.

"A leviathan?"

"No, far worse than that. It has killed countless leviathans." My mouth falls open, and I have to spit out briny water. I think of the dream I had where my father's ship was pulled under the sea. I had seen a brief glimpse of the creature that pulled him down.

"What does it look like? Is it red, with long tentacle arms?" She looks at me uncertainly, and I know the answer is yes.

"We call it the Rimorosa," she says. "It is ancient. It is unstoppable." I can see from her eyes that she doesn't want to say any more. But I still need to figure out a plan. I think back to the submersibles in the Deeplight. My father must have gotten in one. Did it take him to the Forbidden City? If so, there must be a way in.

"How do the sentinels get in and out of the Forbidden City?" I ask.

"There is only one way in, but it is an impossible journey."

"Impossible? How can the sentinels make it in?"

"The entrance lies beneath the seafloor, on the other side of three impassable lands. Believe me when I tell you that no living thing will survive the journey." Her eyes fall and her face looks pained. "My father was the last one of us to try." I put my hand on top of hers. I want to say something to make it better, but I know that nothing will.

I sit with her in silence for a long while. Her eyes are closed. She is tired and weak and needs to rest. I ask her one last thing.

"Will you please tell me your name?" She opens her eyes the tiniest bit and smiles.

"My real name is very long. Nobody has said it in a long time." She is quiet for a moment. It must be hard for her to speak, but her voice is warm and sincere. "When I was young, I met a human girl who looked a lot like you." Her eyes close again. She squeezes my hand gently. "She called me Cara. She said that it means *friend*. You can call me that, if you like."

"Cara, my name is Merryn. Get some rest. I'll keep guard over the cave."

"Merryn," she says softly. "Even your names are similar. The other girl's name was Meara." She closes her eyes.

I hold her hand for a while, a wave of confused feelings rushing through my head.

My mother's name was Meara.

*   *   *   *   *   *

ara and my mother knew each other. Jumbled questions race through my head. There are so many things I want to know. Just then, I hear a yelping noise from outside and I peer out of the cave entrance. Swish is watching something in the distance. I swim out, and the long white beam of a Fomori sentinel passes right over my face. Through the blinding light of the beam I can see the sentinel tilting down toward me. I have only a moment to react.

I dive forward, underneath the sentinel, forcing it to turn away from the cave entrance. I swim straight upward, knocking my head against its smooth, metal underbelly. If I can just stay in its blind spot I may be able to buy some time. The sentinel turns to the left, then to the right, sweeping its beam through the coral in search of me. I take a deep breath from the zephyr whelk as I try to plan my next move.

Abruptly, the sentinel turns back around and shines its beam into the cave entrance.

"No!" I scream, bubbles flying up in front of my eyes. With a quick kick of my legs, I flip myself back toward the rear of the sentinel. I grab onto its wide fan-like rudder with both hands and kick my legs as hard as I can, driving its tail downward and its nose up into the air. I can feel it wrestling with me, trying to turn back around, but I hold on tight, refusing to let it turn toward the cave.

Suddenly the sentinel is lit up, its hull becoming a brilliant gleaming gold. Another beam is shining on me from behind. I turn around just in time to see the other sentinel closing in, its torpedo tubes aimed straight at me. I see the puff of bubbles out of the corner of my eye as I dive down. The torpedo misses me and slams into the other sentinel. A blast of water knocks me against the rock wall above the cave as a shower of shining golden fragments pours down all around me. Something heavy hits me in the back, taking my breath away.

Still shaken by the blast, I try to swim toward the second sentinel. If I can just reach its rudder . . .

But it's too late. The sentinel backs up and lowers its torpedo tubes straight at me. There's nowhere to hide. I close my eyes, bracing for the blast.

I wince as I hear a loud crunch of metal. When I open my eyes, I see Swish has bitten into the side of the sentinel and is shaking it back and forth in his mouth. Splinters of gold fly in all directions as Swish tears through it as if it were made out of paper.

Swish swims back toward me as the last metal scraps of the deadly sentinel drift harmlessly down to the seafloor. I wrap my arms around his neck in a hug. He licks my face with his giant scratchy tongue.

I've made up my mind now. I have to try to make it to the Forbidden City to stop the sentinels. I can only hope my father made it there safely as well, and we'll be reunited there.

Back in the cave, Cara has her body curled around the eggs, trying to protect them. The seahorse is floating at the entrance, standing guard. He must have known that he would have been torn to shreds by the sentinel, but he stayed there anyway.

"You're very brave," I tell him. He lowers his head a little bit. "I can see why Cara cares so deeply for you." It may have been my imagination, but for a moment I thought the light inside him glowed a little bit brighter.

I swim to a thick patch of kelp and cut the longest strands I can, hanging them over the cave entrance to camouflage it. Then I search through the coral and bring back twelve more scallops, laying them down at the floor of the cave. Through the kelp, I call softly to Cara.

"I'm going to try to reach the Forbidden City now."

"No! I can't let you . . ." Cara's voice sounds weak and frail.

"If you lead me to the entrance of the impassable lands, I may die along the way. But if you don't, I will definitely die in search of it," I say. She is quiet. Her face looks grave, but I can see some of the color has come back. I think she's going to be okay. She lifts her head and turns toward the seahorse. Without words, she has said something to him. He swims through curtains of kelp, and points his nose toward the south. He's going to lead me. Cara's voice is so soft now I can barely hear her.

"You're going to find him, Merryn. I can see it."

I feel a lump in my throat as I wave good-bye to her through the kelp.

Swimming back to my sub, I climb through the hatch and turn toward the south. The seahorse leads us out of the Seagarden and over the rolling sandy dunes of the seabed. He stops above a wide rocky fissure in the ground. The fissure leads down into absolute darkness.

"Thank you," I say to the seahorse. "I know Cara will be safe with you at her side." He bows his head to me and swims back the way we came.

I turn to Swish. He waves his tail back and forth excitedly, ready for more adventure.

"I'm sorry, Swish," I say. "I have to do this part alone." He follows alongside me as I sail toward the fissure. I turn back and force myself to use a harsher tone. "Stay! Stay here, Swish. It's too dangerous in there." He makes a whimpering sound and looks at me with big doleful eyes. "No," I tell him firmly. He whimpers again.

I'm trying to make my voice strong and commanding, but it's taking everything I have to keep from crying. Swish has been my source of comfort and companionship down here, and it pains me to have to say good-bye. I know he just wants to help me, but I would never forgive myself if something happened to him in there.

I flip the sub, open the hatch, and swim out, giving him one last hug.

"Once I find my father, I'll come back and we'll play tag all day long," I whisper, hoping he doesn't notice that my voice is trembling. "I promise."

I climb back into the sub. The last things I see are Swish's big yellow eyes watching me pleadingly as I descend into the darkness.

12

THE IMPASSABLE LANDS

The fissure extends downward, hundreds of feet below the seafloor. The gap between the wide smooth rock walls grows even wider, and at last I see a glow below me. I navigate down below the fissure and into a long cavern where the floor bubbles with orange molten rock.

The cavern stretches on endlessly. Plumes of boiling liquid rock erupt like fountains from the floor, lighting up the rocky walls. These are the magma storms, the first of the impassable lands. I remember the name from one of my father's songs. We used to pretend that the floor of my bedroom was covered in hot magma, and I would leap from pillow to pillow to make it to safety. I'd close my eyes and imagine the lavafalls pouring down all around me. It seemed like such a fantastical and beautiful place. But now, as I stare out at the fiery gauntlet ahead of me, I feel nothing but dread.

I imagine my father, somewhere on the other side of the impassable lands.

For a moment I see him. His hat is gone, his eyes are wide, and his dark hair waves in the water. Something is pulling him down, deeper and deeper. His arms are reaching out. He's grasping for something . . . it looks like a glowing yellow balloon . . . and then the vision is gone.

At first I think that my mind is just playing tricks on me, envisioning my greatest fears. But somehow I know my father still needs my help.

I sail forward into the cavern. Searing jets of magma shoot up in front of me, spreading out into sprays of molten red globules that rain down from the ceiling. I dodge to the left, then down, then back to the right, to avoid the glowing balls of magma that billow up all around me. Speeding forward, I narrowly avoid a hail of burning rock as a chunk of ceiling breaks apart and splashes into the river of fire below.

Streams of burning rock pour down from above me like bright orange waterfalls, boiling the water all around them. The walls of my sub are burning hot. Scalding sprays of water shoot through the seams in the sub's exterior, stinging my arms and face. My hands are blistering. The handlebars feel like they've been inside an oven. Sweat is pouring down from my hair and into my eyes so I can barely see. My sub is starting to tear apart at the seams.

I dive down toward the floor as a great fountain of lava arcs across the entire cavern. There's a tiny gap between the boiling floor and the falling sheet of molten rock; I race the sub toward it. I feel a blast of searing heat as I shoot through the gap. The lava crashes down like an avalanche behind me.

My submarine is knocked sideways by the blast of boiling water. The world is a blur of raining fire as I spin around out of control. When I finally stop spinning, I am facing backward, looking out at the raging fiery storm. Below me, the floor is dark solid rock. The scalding sprays of water have stopped.

I'm on the other side of the magma storms.

The cavern widens and slopes downward. There is no light except for the yellow beam from the front of my sub. The cavern's silence and stillness is unsettling—I know there must be danger nearby, but I have no idea what it is.

The ground ahead of me is jagged and white, a stark contrast to the dark rock of the cavern walls. I move forward cautiously, and then stare in horror as I realize what I am seeing.

The floor is a giant pit of bones. Enormous bleached-white bones, bigger than any I have ever seen. They look like the skeletons of legendary serpents, some more than a hundred feet long. *These are the bones of leviathans.*

I stop pedaling and look out across the vast empty cavern. There is no hint of movement.

I shudder to think of what could have killed this many leviathans. And is it still lurking silently in the darkness ahead of me?

My eyes begin to adjust to the darkness. The vault of bones stretches out in front of me like barren white desert, daring me to cross it. I feel a strange pang of sorrow as I think of the great majestic creatures that died here. What brought them all to this one place? My father once told me that the leviathan breeding grounds lay beyond the magma storms—they could make it through the bursts of lava because their armored scales are impervious to heat. Are these the remains of entire generations of leviathans? I think back to Swish's eyes as I left him behind, all alone in the sea. Is he the last of his kind, just like the merrow?

I'm about to push forward when something catches my eye. There is a faint white beam of light cutting diagonally through the water right in front of me. It's barely wider than a blade of grass and so faint that it is nearly impossible to see. It's only because my eyes have had time to adjust that I can see it at all.

At first I want to sail toward it to get a better look, but the eerie silence of the cavern has made me wary. After flipping the sub over, I pop out of the hatch and swim upward alongside the hair-like beam of light, careful not to touch it. As I reach the rough rocky wall of the cavern, I can see that the light is coming through a tiny slit in the rock. Carefully swimming along the wall, I discover more beams. The wall is

No, I don't think I can outrun them. But I have another idea.

I swim up toward the ceiling, carefully weaving between the threads of light, toward the first of the turrets. It has the signature golden clockwork design of the Fomori. The shiny turret barrel rotates inside a sturdy trapezoid-shaped gold frame filled with intricately ticking gears and sliding levers. I look over each moving part, carefully examining how each gear, axle, and lever are connected. It's a truly impressive piece of machinery, but it has one glaring weakness. There are two large powerful gears connected by a single small one. The small one is attached to an axle with a tiny screw.

With the tip of my coral knife, I loosen the screw and pull out the tiny gear. The two large gears slide together, grinding against each other as they try to pull in opposite directions. There is a loud groan of twisting metal as the axles bend and the gears tear through though the turret's housing. With a loud *clang*, the whole turret flies apart, sending the gears, levers, and turret barrel tumbling toward the bed of bones below.

I move on to the next two turrets, carefully dismantling them. I search the whole ceiling of the cavern to make sure I haven't missed any, then pry another rock from the wall. I throw the rock deep into the center of the cavern and watch it fall quietly down until it disappears behind the ribs of a leviathan skeleton.

Now that I've cleared the path of danger, I climb back into the sub and sail forward through the cavern.

That was two impassable lands, I think, as the last of the bones disappear beneath me.

The cavern continues on, wide and straight, with no apparent danger in sight. I pass by dark mouths of caves that lead into winding tunnels. I imagine each tunnel enters a different undiscovered world. In different circumstances, I'd be tempted to follow one, just for a little bit, to see how far it goes.

A long and piercing howl emanates from a cave ahead of me and echoes through the walls of the cavern. A giant eel emerges from that direction, swims across the cavern, and disappears into a tunnel on the other side. It seemed to pay no attention to me at all. Somehow this unsettles me more than if the eel had attacked. It's terrifying to think that some unspeakable danger is lurking nearby, and I have no idea what it is.

Just as I am beginning to wonder if the final impassable land was just a myth, I sail out of the cavern and find myself in endless open water. There is no ceiling and no floor. Vertical rock walls enclose the seemingly bottomless span, forming a giant pillar of water. Peering down into the darkness, I feel like the jaws of a giant beast are rising up to swallow me.

Jutting out from cylindrical walls are golden metal struts. They form a connected lattice like the framework of a bridge. Based on their size and the number of struts, they must be supporting something truly massive. Is the Forbidden City right above me?

As I sail upward through the lattice of golden struts, my feelings of anticipation and excitement vanish in an instant. The white beams of Fomori sentinels sweep through the water above me. Hiding out of sight, I count the beams. When I get to thirteen I stop counting. I'd be lucky to make it past a single sentinel. Getting past more than thirteen will take much more than luck.

One of the sentinels dives down toward me, its beam sweeping through the water. It's too dangerous to wait here. I sail back down to the cavern to think.

And then I see a brief glimpse of something orange disappearing into the mouth of a cave below me. I sail closer, out of curiosity, but there's only a pile of metal scraps and assorted junk, tied up with rope. Among the junk are a cracked clay vase, a tattered sailor's hat, and the broken claw of a Fomori sentinel. I pause for a moment, wondering who would have bothered collecting miscellaneous junk from the sea and why they would leave it down here. Then I look closer at the hat. It looks just like mine, except the anchor is tilted sideways so that it looks like an *E*. E for Eirnin. *It's my father's hat.*

I flip the sub and swim out the hatch to grab the hat, but the whole bundle of scraps suddenly lurches away from me. An orange claw snaps in front of my face, nearly pinching my nose. In front of me is the biggest hermit crab I have ever seen. His body is the size of a large dog and his claws look powerful enough to snap me in half. Shiny black eyes poke out on long orange eyestalks from beneath the pile of scraps he carries on his back. He snaps his claws at me two more times, warning me to back off from his collection of treasures.

"I'm sorry," I tell him sincerely. "I didn't see you. So you collect treasures too?" He snaps his claw at my hand, trying to keep me away. I look at my father's hat, tied up among the rusted gears and odd-looking metal scraps. It makes me happy to know that he made it here. I hold out hope that he's in the Forbidden City already.

The crab is watching me intently, sidling back and forth in the mouth of the tunnel. He must think he looks scary, but to me he's kind of cute. I look up at his bundle of scraps, wondering where he managed to find all those things. An idea pops into my head—a way to get past the sentinels.

"Would you be willing to make a trade?" I ask the hermit crab, pulling one of the gold coins out of my pocket and holding it up. His eyes fixate on it immediately. "It's pretty, isn't it? Much prettier than all those old rusty scraps, right?" He slowly reaches out his claw toward the coin, but I pull it back. "No, no, no, I said *trade*. You have to give me something in return."

The crab lowers the bundle and scuttles two steps back, offering to let me pick whatever I want. I set the coin down in front of him and he eyes it greedily, tapping it with his claw as if he wants to make sure it's real.

"I just need a few things, if that's okay," I tell him. I pick up the broken sentinel claw, a couple of gears, and a few odd but potentially useful scraps of metal. "Will you trade the coin for these?" I ask. "You can keep my father's hat. I think he would understand, and he'd be grateful that you helped me."

The crab looks at the items I have selected, then back at the shiny coin, then finally at me. He picks up the coin and quickly backs away from me, afraid I might change my mind and snatch it back.

"It's all yours," I assure him. I swim back to the sub, holding my newly bartered treasures tightly in one arm. "Thank you for your help!" I call to the crab as I duck inside the hatch.

Inside the sub, I pick up my tools and set to work. I have a plan. It's risky and dangerous and maybe even downright crazy, but it's a plan.

13

THE FORBIDDEN CITY

orking as fast as I can, I hammer each piece of scrap metal into shape. None of them is a perfect fit for what I need, but with a little bending, twisting, and hammering I can get them close enough. I roll a thin piece of metal into a makeshift gear axle and bend another to be a hand lever. I hammer a sharp rock against the sub's roof to make tiny holes for the bolts, and a thin slit for the lever arm. I quickly slide each piece into place to stop the spray of water pouring inside.

The parts are starting to come together, one by one. I take a look at the progress with a mixture of pride and uncertainty. The gears are rusty, and there are no screws to keep their levers in place. The whole contraption is only barely holding together at all. But I don't need it to be perfect. I only need it to work for a few minutes.

I reach up to the ceiling and gently pull the hand lever. I grin as I see the segmented claw arm stretch out. I yank the lever all the way back, and the metal claw slams shut. The bolts on the roof rattle where the claw's arm is connected, but it seems to be holding tight. Well, tight *enough*, at least.

I sail back out of the cavern and look at the circling sentinels above me. I have one chance to make this work.

Moving up along the side of the wall, I watch the sweeping beams of light on their endless patrols. I wait for just the right moment. When the beams are all pointed away from the wall above me, I sail up and yank a large loose rock from the wall with the claw. I struggle to force the sub upright as the weight of the rock pitches it forward. As the sentinel beams turn back toward me, I pull back on the lever, but nothing happens.

Three sentinel beams are approaching. They'll see me at any second! I grip the lever with both hands and yank it with all my might. The arm pitches forward and hurls the rock through the water, slamming into one of the sentinels and sending it spinning around. Five sentinels all turn toward the rock and chase it as it sinks down through the trench. I hear their torpedo shots firing at the rock as they go.

That worked almost too well, but four more sentinels are patrolling in a figure-eight pattern higher above me. Beyond them it looks like there are at least another four—no, five. But as long as I can keep distracting them faster than the other ones can return, I should be fine.

I pull another chunk of rock from the wall. It's about half the size of the first one, so it doesn't throw me off balance as badly. I follow the pattern of the sentinels above me, again carefully waiting for the right moment. When the nearest sentinel is just starting to pass by, I yank the lever, and the stone sails through the water and slams into the top of the sentinel with a satisfying *clank*. But rather than bouncing forward, the stone ricochets upward and back toward me.

I watch, frozen in horror, as all nine sentinels turn

their beams and follow the rock straight toward me. There's nowhere I can go. I'm completely surrounded by them. I remain motionless, hoping that they might turn back around. But they don't.

The first torpedo launches. I dive down as it slams into the wall behind me, and the blast sends me spinning around out of control. I pull the claw lever, trying to grab onto anything I can. The claw sinks into the tail of one of the sentinels, jerking me to a stop. I'm about to release it when I have an idea. I pull the lever back even harder, forcing the claw to bite down harder into the sentinel's tail. Its diving plane, the fin-like part of the tail that lets it go up or down, is jammed upward. The sentinel is forced into an uncontrollable dive, pulling my sub down with it.

I'm being tugged straight down into the endless maw of the trench. Sentinel beams sweep all around me as they give chase from behind. They're going to fire at any moment. There's only one thing I can do.

I force open the hatch and dive out. The sentinels race past me into the darkness below. I see the torpedoes fire, one after the other. There is a bright flash below me. My submarine is blown into a million tiny fragments.

I feel a painful knot in my stomach. I take a short gasping breath through the zephyr whelk. My body is shaking. There's no time to think right now—I just have to move. I swim upward. I block everything else out. All that matters is swimming upward as fast as I can go. The water above me is dark. The sentinels are all below me. I have a few seconds at most. Keep going . . . keep going . . .

The light of a sentinel beam sweeps up past me, through the water on my right, illuminating a ceiling of gold above me. The metal struts widen as they stretch up to the ceiling, as if they are holding it up. At the center of the ceiling is a circular opening of water. I swim straight up toward it, just as the sentinel's beam sweeps over me.

I maneuver into the opening and up through a wide cylindrical tube. I hear a clanking of metal and look down to see that the bottom of the tube has closed behind me. I'm safe from the sentinels for now, but where am I? Is this the entrance to the Forbidden City?

Above me, a hole forms at the center of the ceiling. The hole widens as I approach, and brilliant yellow light shines down on my face, forcing me to shield my eyes. I feel like I've walked out of a dark cave and am looking straight into the midday sun.

I swim up toward the light, and my head emerges into air. I climb out of the tube and turn around in astonishment.

I'm standing in the middle of an entire city made of gold. Pointed spires of buildings tower high above me like a golden forest. Walkways paved with gold zigzag and branch between the gleaming golden walls. Archways and buttresses stretch between the buildings. An immense dome of glass arches over the building tops. Beyond that is the great empty darkness of the sea.

At the edges of the city, the glass dome walls are lined with forty-foot-tall golden gears, each in slow and steady motion. Four tall cylindrical glass tubes, filled with water, run through the center of the city from floor to ceiling. Pumps inside the tubes keep the water in constant motion. Are these gears and tubes used to filter air out of the water?

As I walk through the city, I am stunned at the beauty and wealth all around me. There is more gold in this city than I thought could have existed in all the world. Tall piles of gold coins are pushed up against walls, as if they ran out of places to put them. But where are the Fomori? What could have happened to them to make them abandon such riches?

I think back to what Cara said about the Rimorosa . . . a great ancient beast more powerful than any leviathan. If the Fomori had captured it and even controlled it, could it have turned on them? Maybe they didn't abandon the city after all. Maybe, after so many years of pillaging the sea, the most deadly of all its creatures fought back and destroyed them. Still, it's strange that the city seems to have been abandoned without any kind of struggle.

And where is my father? There is no sign of him anywhere. My submarine is destroyed, and I have no idea where to go next or what to do.

I kick a pile of coins in frustration, watching them scatter and roll across the gleaming golden walkway. I would trade all this gold just for the tiniest hint of where to look for my father.

I follow the winding walkways through the tall buildings until I reach an open garden at what seems to be the center of the dome. There are canals built into the floor, little rivers that travel through the city. They intersect in a shallow pool within the garden, where arching fountains of water take turns shooting up into the air and sending sparkling jewel-drops of water raining back down. Inside the canals, golden clockwork seahorses swim along, busily attending to some invisible task.

Looking closer, there is something different about these seahorses. Cara's seahorse was lit from within by a pulsing white glow that these seahorses don't have. Their movements are more stiff and precise, and they don't seem to be alive and aware of me the way Cara's seahorse was. Now I wish I had asked her how she became friends with it. There must be a bigger story that she didn't tell me.

I follow one of the seahorses through a canal, away from the garden. It seems to move with a purpose, as if it has a job to do. Do the seahorses keep the whole city running? Something must be making the repairs to the machines and keeping the pumps active. And if so, there must be some location in the city that controls all the machinery. Maybe my father came to the same conclusion and has already found it.

The seahorse leads me through golden city streets, along winding canals merging with larger canals and then splitting off again. Finally, it takes me into a low-ceilinged tunnel at the edge of the city. At the end of the tunnel, the canal empties into a deep circular pool. The walls of the pool are covered in little golden switches. The seahorse moves from spot to spot along the wall, flicking the tiny switches with its nose. This must be some kind of control center for the whole city. Maybe there's even a way to disable the sentinels from here.

I dive into the pool and look around the walls, searching for some pattern to the switches. If my father has been here, he must have done the same thing I am doing now. Did he flip one of the switches? And if so, where did he go? I look down at the golden floor. I would guess that it leads back into the open trench beneath the city.

The switches are arranged in long densely packed columns with no symbols or any other indication of their purpose. The seahorse stops flipping the switches and turns to me.

"I don't suppose you could show me what these do?" I ask with a smile, gesturing to the switches. The seahorse just turns away from me and moves to another column, switching them all down one by one. I hear a grating of metal and look up to see the golden iris ceiling closing. A moment later the floor slides up below me, revealing the endless trench. I look at the seahorse with a feeling of betrayal. "Did you do that?" There is no sign of the sentinels, at least. Maybe they are patrolling deeper in the trench.

The seahorse is just floating there, watching me. It makes me a little uncomfortable, but I'll just have to ignore him and stay focused. I scan the columns of switches and swim over to one. I could start by flipping all the switches in the column just to see what happens. But as I'm reaching for the first one, I feel a swell of water pushing up from below.

I look down to see a huge red tentacle reaching up. Before I can move, it wraps around me and pulls me down into the darkness!

I'm sinking so fast I can barely see. My ribs feel like they are going to crack from the pressure of the tentacle's grip. The beams of sentinels and glints of golden struts fly past me and disappear.

This must be the Rimorosa. This is the creature that sank my father's ship. I struggle to free myself from its merciless grip, but the undulating tentacles just propel me farther into the depths.

14

THE RIMOROSA

'm enveloped in blackness now, except for the glimmer of yellow-orange glowkelp bulbs along the walls of the trench, their lights streaking by me like shooting stars. I feel the tentacle loosen its grip for a moment and I am able to take a quick breath through the zephyr whelk. For a moment I see a glimpse of the Rimorosa's face. Its head is like that of an octopus but is covered with eyes. I notice a gold band around its skull, like a helmet. Maybe that was how the Fomori controlled it. And is that what allows the Rimorosa to control the sentinels now?

The glowkelp bulbs fly past as the ancient beast pulls me farther down into the depths. I wriggle back and forth, pushing as hard as I can against the constricting arm. I make it only a few inches before the tentacle squeezes even tighter.

But those few inches are enough to allow me to reach the handle of my coral knife. As I pull it out, a second tentacle wraps around my head and neck. I can feel its suction cups against my face. Now I can't see, and I have no way to breathe. My fingernails dig into the suction cups along the tentacle at my waist, trying to pry them free, but it's no use.

Gripping the knife with both hands, I blindly stab it into the tentacle at my waist. I hear a piercing screech as the coral blade sinks into one of the suction cups. Both the tentacles loosen, and I kick my way free. I swim upward as fast as I can go. One of the tentacles brushes my leg, but I slip out of its grasp before it can get hold of me.

I swim toward the wall, sliding through a web of tangled vines and into a long narrow crack, just big enough for me squeeze into sideways. I hold my breath as the tentacle arms tear through the vines and try to pry me out. I can feel the suction cups tickling my shins, so I wedge myself in deeper. The tentacles try again and again to grasp hold of me, but they aren't able to get a solid grip.

At last, the tentacles retreat and the Rimorosa disappears down into the depths.

I listen for any movement from below, but all is silent. I swim out of the crack, feeling the tendrils of the vines reaching toward me. As I shake them off and push away from the wall, I see what they are. The walls are covered in thick layers of strangleclaw kelp. Its bulbs may look pretty, but if it gets its barbed, claw-like hooks in me it will pull me all the way to the bottom of the trench.

That's why the Rimorosa left. It wasn't giving up; it was merely waiting for the kelp to grab me and bring me down to it. *How much time do I have before it comes back to check on me?* I swim up through the trench, the glowing kelp bulbs forming a cylinder of tiny lights leading upward along the walls of the trench.

As I swim farther up, I see a long dark swath in the lights, running vertically down the wall. It looks like a column of darkness in a starry sky. Remembering what my father once said about using the kelp bubbles to breathe, I swim toward the bottom, where the patch of darkness ends. There, tangled and still amid the vines, is the body of a man. It's my father.

I race toward him. His eyes are closed—he looks like he's sleeping. A deflated kelp bulb is clenched in his fingers. Was he breathing through the kelp bulbs as the strangleclaw pulled him farther down into the trench? How long has he been down here? There must have been more than a hundred kelp bulbs in the dark swath above him; he could have survived for quite a while on them.

I grab his arm and shake him, but he doesn't move. I take off the zephyr whelk necklace and hang it around his neck, putting the shell up to his lips. He still doesn't move.

"Breathe!" I yell. I feel the strangleclaw wrapping around me and tightening. My father's eyes stay closed. The kelp pulls me lower, tugging me away from him. I reach toward him and grab onto his boot as I am pulled away again.

He's too far away for me to reach now. His body is still. The zephyr whelk hangs at his neck.

I am too late.

There is a rush of moving water from below. I turn to see the Rimorosa swimming up through the trench, straight toward me. Before I can even move, it yanks me out of vines and grips me in one of its giant red arms.

With another arm, it grasps my father's body and it pulls us both back down into the depths. My father's arms flail gently in the water beside me. I reach for his hand and hold it tightly in mine, knowing I won't be able to hold my breath much longer.

And then he opens his eyes.

His eyes widen in disbelief when he sees me and then quickly fill with horror. I gesture to the zephyr whelk around his neck, then put my hands to my mouth to show what to do. He holds it up and takes a deep breath. He looks at me incredulously. There are a million things he wants to say and no time to say them. He takes off the necklace and stretches it out to me. I take a deep breath.

We pass the zephyr whelk back and forth as the Rimorosa pulls us deeper into the trench. My father starts to say something, but I shake my head and hold my finger to my lips. We're going to have to conserve our breaths. Maybe when the Rimorosa comes to a stop, we'll have a chance to escape.

From high above us, a terrible roar echoes down through the trench. An immense shadow engulfs the lights as it descends toward us. There is another great roar, and I see an enormous gaping mouth, filled with a thousand saber-size teeth. *It's a queen leviathan*, the most feared creature in all the sea.

Her great mouth lunges toward us. I grip my father's hand and close my eyes as the giant teeth gnash down. I feel the Rimorosa's tentacles loosen their grip, and I open my eyes.

The leviathan has bitten into the other creature. My father pulls me away from the tentacles, and we swim up alongside the thrashing serpentine body of the leviathan. The Rimorosa has wrapped its tentacles around the head and neck of the leviathan as the leviathan struggles to attack again. The two are locked in a desperate struggle—and neither seems to have an advantage.

My father tugs me away from the battling beasts. Two yellow eyes are coming toward us.

Protectively, my father plants himself in front of me, but I recognize the eyes instantly. It's Swish. I look back down at the queen leviathan, still battling the Rimorosa.

"Swish, is that . . . is that your mother?" I ask him. My father looks from me to Swish and back again. "I'll explain it all later," I tell him, taking a breath from the zephyr whelk. I give Swish a big hug. He swims above us and wiggles his tail, as if asking us to grab on. "It's okay," I say to my father, and we both grab hold of Swish's tail.

Swish pulls us up out of the trench and into the cavern where I came in. From down below I hear another roar, and the giant leviathan flies up through the trench, with the Rimorosa chasing close behind it. Swish makes a whimpering sound as he looks toward the trench. I squeeze his fin, trying to console him.

Loud crashes of metal and rock echo through the trench, and I look at my father, suddenly realizing what is happening. The leviathan is destroying the metal struts that support the Forbidden City.

The sound builds to a thunder. The leviathan swoops down into the cavern as the weight of an entire city comes crashing down behind her. I see a glimpse of the red tentacles of the Rimorosa, but a moment later it is buried beneath an avalanche of gold. All the riches of the Forbidden City disappear out of sight into the infinite abyss of the trench.

I turn to the queen leviathan. Swish's mother. She looks like she came away unhurt. I think of the giant skeletons of leviathans that I passed in the cavern. She must have known she was taking a great risk to come here. Swish rubs his cheek against his mother's face.

"Thank you," I say. "We can never repay you for that."

She rolls her back toward us, revealing the spines along the back of her head.

My father looks at me in disbelief. Is she offering us a ride?

We grab onto the spines, and the leviathan carries us out of the trench, up into the open sea where the Forbidden City once was. She takes us higher and higher, until we can see the distant streaks of the sun's rays above us.

And then we are above the water, sailing toward the dark brown cliffs in the distance.

We're going home.

15

SEASHELL SOUP

"Wake up, Dandelion," my father calls to me. "We need to get an early start if we're going to bring anything home for Fergus tonight." I hurriedly get dressed and meet him in the kitchen. There's a plate of pancakes waiting for me on the table. My father has drawn a seahorse on them with honey.

"Mmmmm! Who knew seahorses were so tasty?" I say between bites. My father sits down to eat his own stack of pancakes, pouring the honey on top. "Guess we don't have to worry about sweets attracting leviathans anymore, right?"

"Maybe I should bring a little extra honey in the boat, just in case," he says, stroking his chin as if he's thinking about it intently.

We finish up breakfast and walk down the cliff steps. My father has put long wooden planks over the gap, but he still reminds me to be careful as we cross it. Down at the shore, Fergus is waiting, perched on the bow of our new boat. Well, not *new* exactly, but it's new to us. We sold one of the coins I found in the Seagarden and used the money to buy the boat. There was even enough left over to buy a whole new set of paints, and new seeds for my garden.

As we sail out to sea, we take turns telling each other of our adventures below the sea. And this time the stories are real. My father tells me how he was sucked into the current and pulled into the Deeplight. He climbed into one of the gold-and-glass submersibles, hoping to reach the surface. But there was no way to pilot it, and it instead took him through a golden iris-shaped gate and into a tube in the top of the glass dome of the Forbidden City. *That makes sense*, I think. Only the Fomori's vessels would be able to use that entrance. The impassable lands were like a secret heavily guarded back door.

Once in the city, my father searched for a way to escape and reach the surface. He stayed there for many hours, at one point trying to smash the dome itself and swim to the surface. He found the same pool of switches that I had later found and was captured by the Rimorosa. He must have lost his hat on the way down, and it floated down to where the hermit crab found it.

As the Rimorosa dragged him down, he grabbed onto the kelp vines along the wall and pulled himself free of the tentacles. But he became trapped in the tangles of the strangleclaw, and it pulled him gradually downward through the trench. He used the kelp bulbs to breathe, as infrequently as he could bear.

He must have been down there for a few hours before I found him. Eventually he could no longer reach any more bulbs, and he blacked out. I must have found him just after that. Even with all the things that went wrong, I can't help but feel that we were very lucky.

We check the nets for fish. We've had a good catch so far. Maybe the fish are starting to come back! It's my turn to share a story, so I tell my father about Cara. I describe the house she grew up in, with the seashell drawings on the wall. I tell him about the cave of eggs that shined like rubies. And, finally, I tell him that she once had a friend named Meara. He looks off toward the distant cliffs and is quiet for a long time.

"I think we've caught enough for today," he says. "Let's head back a little early." From the sound of his voice, I already know where we are going.

Back at the shore, we give Fergus three of our biggest fish and climb back up the steps. In the fields beyond my garden, at the edge of the cliffs, my father and I pick wild orchids. We use a needle and thread to turn them into a pretty purple necklace, just like my mother used to do. Then we walk up the old overgrown path that runs alongside the sea until we reach the grassy hill at the highest point of the cliffs. This is where past generations of my family have been buried. There are graves here that are more than three hundred years old. Standing tall, at the very edge of the cliff, is my mother's stone.

We lay the necklace of flowers gently down on top of her grave. We stand, listening to the waves of the sea, as the smell of the orchids embraces us.

The sun sinks below the cliffs and we turn to walk back down the hill. As we pass one of the worn old stones, something catches my eye. The name and date are too weathered to read, but there is an unmistakable engraving of a tall stone tower with a light shining at the top.

My ancestors were Fomori. But why did my mother keep that a secret? Was she ashamed of it? I wish I could tell her about Cara; how she's all grown up, how she still remembers my mother's friendship. I keep thinking of her lying in the cave, protecting her eggs. Is she safe now? Are the sentinels all gone? If I don't find out, I'm always going to wonder.

I hold my father's hand as we stroll along the path.

"How about I make a great big pot of seashell soup?" he asks. When he sees my confused expression he quickly adds, "To go with the fish, of course." But now I understand that seashell soup is more than just a last resort meal to him. It's a reminder that we made it. We survived. And we did it together.

"That sounds like the most delicious thing ever," I say with a smile. We continue down the hill. I playfully kick a tiny rock, watching as it skitters along the path. I look up at my father's face. His eyes are no longer sad. I squeeze his hand a little tighter. "Dad, I was just wondering one thing."

"What's that?"

"Is it okay if I build another submarine?"

ACKNOWLEDGMENTS

'd like to thank Christina Pulles and Hanna Otero, editors extraordinaire, for their inspiration, creativity, and guidance throughout this journey. I could not have done this without their help.

Many thanks to Theresa Thompson and everyone at Sterling Publishing for believing in this story when it was in its infancy. And thank you to Lorie Pagnozzi, Jo Obarowski, Ardi Alspach, Sari Lampert, Kim Broderick, Terence Campo, and Fred Pagan at Sterling for all your hard work on this project!

Thanks to the GameStop family for their strong support and partnership throughout the entire *Song of the Deep* adventure.

Special thanks to a few individuals from GameStop for their support in making this book come to life: Mark Stanley, Cole Young, Nobie Yamawaki, Matt Stadler, Ashley Acks, Shara Reardon, and Jordan May.

Thank you to the *Song of the Deep* game team and everyone at Insomniac Games whose art, engineering, and ideas turned Merryn's journey into a living, breathing world. This book wouldn't be possible without you. Your talents and hard work not only made this project a reality, but made it a story that I think people will remember and share for years to come.

And thank you to my wife, Clare, who is a source of inspiration to me every day. This book is about what it means to be a hero, and you have always been mine.